Chinaman's Reef Is Ours

IVAN SOUTHALL

Chinaman's Reef Is Ours

ST MARTIN'S PRESS
New York

AFFILIATED PUBLISHERS: Macmillan & Company, Limited,
London—also at Bombay, Calcutta, Madras and Melbourne—
The Macmillan Company of Canada, Toronto.

Contents

CHAPTER ONE

Break It and Beware

THE four big kids—not often dignified by the name of 'teen-agers' at Chinaman's Reef—began drifting away from the shade trees at the fence-line as soon as the small fry came leaping out of the hall. Perhaps that particular human eruption should have ended in a heap of tangled limbs and tear-stained faces at the bottom of the steps, but they were a sure-footed lot. There were only seven of them, all younger than twelve, and out they came like a litter of half-grown pups. Nothing odd; just ordinary; nothing suggesting that it was a Sunday morning any different from the rest.

Kids at Chinaman's Reef, generally speaking, were all a bit wild, all a bit noisy, even on Sundays. They always had been, their fathers and grandfathers before them. When they grew up, if they stayed on at Chinaman's, they'd change. That was the way of it. The grown-ups were rather sad-eyed people trying not to notice decay everywhere around them.

Surprisingly, there were only five small fry that morning. Two were missing, the younger Garretts, Eileen and Larry. Everyone noticed their absence. Chinaman's Reef was that sort of place, almost tribal; anything of note was of note to all. Ronnie Garrett hadn't turned up either and Ronnie was far from unimportant at Chinaman's even though he lived miles out and his father scared other people's kids half to death.

After the small fry, a few seconds behind them as was the rule, came Auntie Sadie Stevenson dressed in black, five feet ten inches tall (probably once nearer six feet), as thin as any human being could reasonably be, but with a presence, full-face, as commanding as a dowager queen. Some might have thought she looked frail, as though the fluids that should have made her body soft had dried up. Others said she lived on her nerves, by sheer will-power, that any woman as fragile as she was should have been dead long ago.

Usually, she stood in the shadow at the top step and raised an arm into the sunlight with one forefinger extended. Her theatrical gesture was a memory that generations of grown-up children had taken with them to the world of roaring cities far away. After a time, of course, they forgot her, or tried to forget her, or smiled tolerantly at themselves for ever having been impressed. Usually she said, counting unnecessarily with her finger (there had never been many of them, after all), 'Everyone here who's going to be here? Good. Come along.' But this morning was different. Her arm went part way up, then suddenly dropped.

The four big kids, waiting to go inside, could almost hear her think, 'Ronnie not here either? I thought I'd not heard the car come along. Why not? Ronnie's not missed a fine Sunday in years. What's happened to the Garretts?'

They heard wrongly because they invented the words for themselves out of what they knew and understood of her. The words might have differed from one to another but the sense was the same. But Auntie Sadie had not posed a question because Ronnie Garrett wasn't there, she had arrived at an instant and passionate answer, as if a blow had been struck at her.

The violence that welled up caught at her breath and hurt her heart and she had to fight it all back because she was afraid she would curse and swear and that would have been awful, perhaps unbelievable. Hate demanded words of its own, and words of that kind she had never used aloud from the day she was born.

Something inside her cried out, 'Don't you care, Mr Garrett? Don't you know what you've done?'

Everything within her became a confusion that frightened her; there were too many thoughts rushing all ways at once; there were too many feelings trying to escape from the certainty that the Garrett children had gone without a goodbye. If they had not gone Ronnie at least would be here. Ronnie always came. Ronnie never missed a Sunday. Though why he came, at sixteen years of age, she was never sure.

'I'll send them away,' Ronnie's father had said, 'you'll not get at me through them. How dare you accuse me of betrayal. Betrayal of what? Of a parasitic place like this, of a bunch of good-for-nothings mending roads hundreds of miles from anywhere that no one needs! Of their children growing up with no hope! The town's dead. It's better buried. You're not the friend of these people here; you're their worst enemy. They're better off in cities. They'll bless the day they shook its dust off their feet.

'Who do you think you are, Miss Stevenson? Santa Claus? God Almighty? Who's paid their wages all these years? Chinaman's Reef hasn't been kept alive by your kind of sentiment, not by fancy talk or Sunday Schools or book groups or pottery classes, but most reluctantly by my Company's money. The Company has been very generous, as you should know, but they've lost patience—after fifty years! Are you surprised?

'I'm sick to death of it, of you, of this place, and of the make-believe of playing the benevolent squire. Fifteen years of it I've had, watching my wife wither up, denying my children their proper chance, trying to fight you legally, fairly, and in a proper way. I'm sick to death of it, Miss Stevenson. If this Company ever had an obligation to Chinaman's Reef it was honoured years ago. You know the wealth that's here, you know where it is, and that it's worth a fortune to this country in foreign exchange. We're going to have that wealth. I warn you, when my children go you can start counting the days.'

She had recoiled physically; she had almost wept in his presence; he had shouted her down.

The four young people, her 'big kids', had left the shade of the peppercorns and were crossing the open ground with an uncertainty that she could see. Time had not stood still while her thoughts had run wild. 'Oh my children, what can I say . . .'

She shrank from them, knowing their doubts, knowing that they had guessed that something was wrong because she had broken the habit of a lifetime. She tried hard to put it right, to get out the words—'Everyone here who's going to be here'— but they wouldn't come; words turned only into a shouting match that went on inside her.

'A lifetime I've given this God-forsaken place, and for what? For a man like Garrett to wipe out overnight. What's the use of *praying* now?'

They were grouping at the foot of the steps, but she wouldn't look down at them. She struggled for composure, but it was terribly, terribly hard. For once in her life she would have taken back her girlhood and started another life, a different one in a different direction, an entirely different life, looking after herself, letting the rest of the world go hang.

They were peering up, four raised faces looking up, healthy kids so like their smaller brothers and sisters leaping away, leaping off. Rugged-looking kids scraped clean rather than sponged clean (with one exception) that you'd expect to see swinging from trees or chopping a hundredweight of wood before breakfast. Their skin had that particular texture, as if rough-worn from scrubbing brushes and weather.

She wouldn't look at them. If any one of them had held her eyes for longer than a moment she would have destroyed with her outburst an image of love and strength that had taken her a lifetime to make. Would they ever have understood the anguish that could drive her to deny not only them, but herself?

'Chinaman's,' she would have cried, 'has any one of you ever thought what it's cost me? I could have joined the trek to the cities like the rest and had all the things I've missed. Things I've missed that you don't even know exist. But I stayed, I stuck it out, because I thought it was what God had the right to expect. And an hour a week I've been given back, if the rain hasn't stopped you, or the measles, or a cold in the head, or some other piffling excuse. In one hour I've tried to make something of you, something extra, something good. In one hour what hope have I had? We're God-forsaken, the lot of us. You go away and hardly ever look back. Now you'll all go, every mother's child of you, and you won't even care.'

They were still there, looking up, dressed in their Sunday best, a slightly uncomfortable, cheap Sunday best; often-washed white cottons and hard-ironed denims a bit frayed at the edges.

'You don't look right, do you? You never have; you never will. Play-acting. Pretending. All dressed up. Suffering out your hour until you can run. Except for you, dear Leah. You're a sweet thing. Sweet and colourless, dear Leah. The youngsters with spirit outgrow me and throw me off.'

They were getting restless.

Shane whispered, 'What's wrong with her? Do you reckon she's sick?'

She heard and deliberately ignored it; to them she seemed only to be looking out over their heads towards the dust-coloured township that crouched so close to the earth among the peppercorns and pines. Chinaman's Reef had crouched there for fifty years, ever since its glory had suddenly ended, crouched there and crumbled brick by brick, perhaps to get out of the sun, perhaps to nurse its strength, perhaps only that it might die undisturbed by the uninterested world that had no further use for it, imagining that the last of Chinaman's wealth had been safely dredged.

Leah turned first, then Shane and Cherry, then Normie turned to look where she looked, but nothing was there to see, nothing new. Nothing was out of place except a few more boards from the walls of the hotel, but the Pride of Ballydoon had been falling for years, railing by railing, balcony by balcony, memory by memory.

Out there somewhere the sounds of the assorted small fry escaped into the background hum. The hum was part of the heat shimmer, the granulated haze that turned distances into mirages, that severed old poppet-heads and trees from the earth and floated them in the sky. 'Listen,' kids sometimes said, 'hear it?' There was nothing to hear, but they heard it just the same, a vast stillness that fed on separate sounds and digested them with a hum of satisfaction. Perhaps that was the way it had been before the white man came like a mole and scarred an ancient plain with heaps and holes. Thousands of years of stillness interrupted for just a little while.

'Shane!'

Auntie Sadie pronounced it *Shorn*, but it sounded choked.

Four heads turned, Shane's with a nervous start.

'Yes, Miss Stevenson.'

But she choked up completely. It was Shane's face that stopped her, a boy's face, perhaps better suited to a twelve-year-old than to a lad going on fifteen. Why was it Shane's name that she had called? Why not Normie? Why not Cherry? They were the ones with backbone. She had been going to say, 'Now listen to me. There's a reason why the Garretts are not here and that reason is something we've got to fight. I doubt if your parents ever will. When we get down to brass tacks they'll not have the heart. "What's the use?" they'll say. "It's bigger than us." But if someone doesn't fight, Chinaman's will be swept from the earth. Will you do *that* much for me? Or are you going to lie down and let it roll over you? Are you going to lose all the little things that count? Every tree, every paving stone, every flower nursed through the heat, every footprint you've ever placed upon the earth?'

But were they the things a woman of seventy-nine could put to children, picking on Shane first, placing the onus on him?

'Yes, Miss Stevenson?'

He was still down there, with a shadow on his face, looking up. Poor Shane, startled and a little pale, searching himself for some forgotten act that might have led Auntie Sadie to single him out, because this was not the way that Sundays went. Auntie Sadie had long ago established a system for everything. 'Habit is our master,' was one of her sayings, 'good habit is a rock in a difficult world. Break it and beware.' Addressing him in that tone of voice at that particular time had nothing to do with the habit of what Sunday mornings were about.

She troubled him, with that glaze over her eyes, with that curiously hard line almost carved into one side of her face. He knew that something was wrong. What had he done?

'You're in charge, Shane,' she said.

He heard, but was astonished, because he had heard nothing like it from her before. She made a statement of it, with brittleness. She told him without calling on extra words that he was to be responsible for good behaviour, that for some extraordinary reason she was not ready to begin Sunday School at the usual hour in the usual way. Shane had never been in charge of anything much before. He wasn't built for authority.

'I'll be back,' she said, and came down the steps and paused in the middle of them. 'You're to go inside. You're to sit quietly.'

'When will you be back, Miss Stevenson?' That came from Normie Muir, naturally enough.

'At any moment, Normie.' Which warned him, bluntly, that she was not in the humour for his sort of fun. 'Sit in my chair, Shane. You're in charge.'

Then she passed between them, away from them, and became a peculiar, angular, stick-like figure in black against a backdrop of brown land, dust-diffused green, and enormously bright sky. It was only face to face that she looked like a dowager queen. Strangers might have laughed at her oddness; even those who knew her sometimes had to smile. 'Don't recall her ever looking younger,' Grandpa Baxter used to say, 'don't see her ever looking older. But she was old when she was young. Only an old head would do what she's done. She's got a broomstick hidden away, I reckon.'

Years ago, when young Shane had first heard those words, he had spent anxious nights at the window of his room waiting for the moonrise behind Auntie Sadie's house. The house sat upon a hillock at the other end of town like a wart on a witch's nose. But he never saw Auntie Sadie in flight on her broomstick, never saw her cross the moon.

'What's going on?' he said. 'Where's she off to?'

'Search me,' said Normie, whose approach to mystery was as honestly uncomplicated as his approach to almost everything. Why spoil an interesting question by worrying it to death? But Leah said, 'Because of the Garretts, do you think?'

'Because of why?' said Shane. 'Because of what about the Garretts?'

'Because they're not here, of course. I mean, they're always here, aren't they?'

'Are they? They don't come when it rains, do they? Maybe they thought it was going to rain.'

The Garretts usually walked home three miles. Mr Garrett was difficult like that; he would bring his children in, but hardly ever called for them afterwards and Mrs Garrett's feelings, if she had any, didn't seem to count. She was known more by rumour than by reputation as a timid little woman who was scared to open her mouth. Her husband might have been rich and all the rest of it, he might have lived in a big house with brick walls and a tennis court, he might have owned Chinaman's Reef from one end of Main Street to the other, but the gentle art of fatherhood seemed to be out of his touch. 'If the children are not prepared to make some effort for themselves,' he said, 'they might as well not go to Sunday School. If they're prepared to face a three-mile walk afterwards that's all right by me. If not, there can't be much worth missing.'

Auntie Sadie was looking back from a short distance down the track. Her arm was raised; her finger was extended.

'That means get up them stairs,' grumbled Normie.

So they went inside.

CHAPTER TWO

Hearts and Hands and Voices

AUNTIE SADIE STEVENSON felt lost, as if Chinaman's Reef were no longer the oasis that appeared (unrealistically) like a fair city over the skyline of the plain when she had been away. Already, in an awful vision, it had turned to dust, already it was a featureless expanse and she wandered in it by herself, a soul lost between worlds, totally betrayed.

Perhaps for too long she had been able to predict what the next day would bring. It would bring back the things of yesterday to live over again, unless for sheer devilment she decided to sleep in. Day would follow day, hens would go broody, goats would have kids, flowers would come in season, and there would always be a few children left. Then one morning she would lie still, like everyone else who had ever lived, and the barking of the dog and the quietness of the house would bring them to the door, the Baxters, the Elliots, the Muirs, the Coopers and perhaps old Dad Murphy if he did not die first. There they would knock. Then they would say, 'She's gone. She's dead.' But that would have been a proper end. This end was not.

Out of sight of the hall she stopped, at a loss. She stopped in the middle of the main street, the street of familiar ghosts, with the Pride of Ballydoon on her right and the derelict blacksmith's shop on her left. They were still there, undeniably there, strangely beautiful in their neglect.

She stopped in full sun, her black garments soaking up the heat, in the ragged gash of sunlight that lay between the shadows of the trees lining the street. Stopped there and cried.

The hall had a musty smell, like old books, and a surprising

depth of gloom that told of years of dust and disuse, years of
slumbering behind yellowed windows and closed doors; too
many years and not enough people. But the kids were used to it.
They didn't really notice. There was scarcely a building in
Chinaman's Reef that hadn't something of the same smell
about it.

Normie dragged a wobbly chair to the window and stepped
up, hoping for a view of Auntie Sadie. He couldn't see a thing
and rubbed vigorously on the glass with the flat of his hand. It
was rough and sticky to the touch.

'Get down,' grumbled Shane, 'you know what she said about
sitting still.'

'Maybe she's gone to ring the Garretts,' Leah suggested—she
took part in conversations at Sunday School more often than
anywhere else—then sat in her usual place, unaware of the
care she took to arrange her frock. Leah was the one completely
feminine girl in miles, the sort who cocked a little finger without
trying and walked 'as if snails were squashing under her feet',
as Normie in a poetic moment had expressed it.

'You can't ring the Garretts, Leah,' Normie said, 'the
number's not listed and not even Ronnie'll crack a peep. You
ought to know that.'

'It's listed now.'

'Come off it, Leah; since when?'

'Since a couple of months ago. It's not in the last phone book
but it'll be in the next.'

'Strike me, they wouldn't tell anyone, would they? Did anyone tell you, Shane? Did anyone tell you, Cherry? What's
happened to Ronnie's old man? Gone social all of a sudden?
I'll bet Auntie Sadie doesn't know.'

'I'll bet she does,' said Cherry from her place at the piano.
'Is there anything Auntie Sadie doesn't know?' Habit found her
turning the hymn book to a well-thumbed page: *Now thank we
all our God, with hearts and hands and voices* . . . Then she swivelled
on her stool for an opinion, eyebrows raised almost to the halo
of white clapped on her head.

'I wish someone had told me,' Normie said. 'I could have
rung Ronnie up. Crikey, that phone box sitting there outside
the Store doing nothin'. I could have been using it.'

'You use it now, don't you?'

Normie pulled a face at Cherry. 'Yeh, but I mean properly.'

'I wish you'd get down off that chair,' Shane growled. 'You're too heavy for it. If you break it there'll be what-oh. You know what she said.'

'She can't see through walls, can she?'

'And you can't see out either. No one'll see through that window for ever and ever. Come on, Normie, get down. I'm in charge. I'm the one who's going to cop it if it breaks, not you.'

'That'd be a real nice change, anyway.' But Normie got down and straddled the chair with his chin over the back of it and beamed cheekily at Cherry. Or perhaps his brightness was a reflection of Cherry's way of adding a touch of light wherever she looked.

'What'll we do?' said Normie.

'Nothing,' said Shane, 'except *sit*.'

'I'll give you an arm wrestle.'

'You won't.'

'I'll give *you* an arm wrestle, Cherry.'

'You try,' growled Shane, 'and I'll flatten you.'

'Strike me,' said Normie, 'this I've got to see.'

'Please,' wailed Shane, 'don't stir anything up. Sit still, Normie. Be a pal. You wouldn't like it if you were in charge.'

Normie pulled another face that made the girls smile. There wasn't much that Normie couldn't do with his face, or with his hands either. He was a big fellow for a boy not quite fourteen. He could have picked Shane up and thrown him a couple of yards, but in fact he wouldn't have laid a finger on him.

'How about playin' us the *Sabre Dance*?' he said to Cherry.

'You can get lost, you can. She'd kill me.'

He giggled. 'That's why I'm askin'. Then we wouldn't have to listen to you practising it, murderin' it every night.'

'Thanks,' said Cherry, 'thank you very much. But you don't have to hang around our front gate, do you! You could stop in your own backyard and do your homework for a change.'

'It's hot in here,' Leah said, with faint embarrassment, because boys didn't stand at her gate, except by accident.

'Is it?' Shane didn't think so. 'No hotter than usual. Maybe it's going to rain.'

'Yeh,' grumbled Cherry, 'next winter. You're a drip, Shane. Rain he says.'

'No, seriously,' Shane said. 'There must be some reason why the Garretts haven't come. They've got a barometer, you know. Maybe it says stormy or something.'

'Yeh, a sun storm.'

There was a general sigh of restlessness.

'I wonder what she's doing,' Leah complained, 'going off like that? I hope she comes back. I mean, you get used to Sunday School, don't you? It's—something to do.' It was Leah's week to read aloud from the Bible and everyone admitted she read well. Leah enjoyed Auntie Sadie's reflective smile of approval. Leah's was a modest sort of pleasure. She hoped, too, to impress Shane.

Normie kicked at a leg of his chair with his heel. 'Go on, Cherry, give it a burl. The *Sabre Dance* or something. I don't mind sufferin'. What do you say, Shane? Are you going to give her permission.'

'I said no, didn't I?'

Cherry struck a discord on the keyboard with her elbows. 'Permission's got nothing to do with it, or *suffering* either. You're a crumb, Normie Muir. I don't play anything for anybody.' But she was itching to. Cherry had a way with the piano, but didn't read music well although there were people who thought she did. Cherry's music was instinctive.

'Do you reckon something's up?' Leah asked.

'Up?'

'Like something *serious*. They don't tell us everything, you know.'

'Who doesn't?'

'Parents.'

'Strike me,' said Normie, 'in our house everybody tells everybody everything, even what you're gettin' for Christmas.'

'You didn't *know* you were getting the rifle.'

'I did. I've got spies. Those horrible little sisters.'

They were becoming impatient, but they respected Auntie Sadie. They might have moaned sometimes, 'Sunday School again,' but always went cheerfully enough. She had asked them to sit, she expected them to behave, and in a way everything about the place suggested her continuing physical presence, the faded prints of religious pictures on the walls, the fancy Biblical texts in old-fashioned type, and the empty 'visitor's chair', always set in place but hardly ever occupied. Any kid from far away was like a major historical event in Chinaman's Reef.

'Go on, Cherry,' Normie urged, 'play us something.'

'She *can't*,' Shane snapped.

'Who says I can't?'

'I do. I'm in charge. It's not my fault she put me in charge. You'll have to put up with it.'

'You'd make a shockin' prefect,' Normie grumbled, 'if ever you get to fifth form remind me not to vote for you, will you? Give him the big stick and he goes crazy. She could play *Onward Christian Soldiers* or something.'

'She blooming well can't.'

'They'd never make him a prefect,' Cherry said, 'they don't make little squirts into prefects.'

Shane flushed. 'You shut up, Cherry Cooper.' (Leah flushed, too, but no one noticed.) 'My mum says I'll be tall, you'll see, I've got big feet.'

'You can say that again. Feet, he calls them. Yards, he means. You'd be tall now if you weren't tucked under so much at the bottom.'

'Get off his back, Cherry,' Normie growled. 'He is in charge, like he says. He can't help it. It's not his fault. And I'm the one that's doin' all the nagging.'

'Aren't we noble,' mocked Cherry.

'She's an awfully long time,' Leah said quickly. 'She hasn't gone home, surely?' Changing subjects to keep the peace was second nature to Leah.

'Yeh,' yelled Normie, 'come on, Auntie Sadie.'

'Don't yell,' shouted Shane. 'Sit down and shut up.'

'I am sittin' down.'

'Crikey,' groaned Shane. 'Play *Onward Christian Soldiers*, Cherry. Play something. But make it holy.'

'No,' said Cherry.

'Look, I'm ordering you to.'

'You don't order me around, Shane Baxter, I'm blowed if you do. If I play anything it's because I want to.'

'Well *want* to, will you!'

'You just can't *want* to do something because someone tells you to, and particularly when you do the telling.'

'Particularly!' His voice became a screech. 'Why *particularly*? What have I done?'

'Golly,' wailed Leah. 'Don't let's fight. We're in Sunday School!'

'Yeah,' said Normie, 'turn it up. Like Leah says, we're in Sunday School.'

'Who's talkin' now?' yelled Shane. 'Who started it? Who stirred it up? Who stirs up everything round here?'

'Please,' cried Leah.

Cherry's hands crashed down on the keys with the opening bars of the *Sabre Dance* and Shane felt suddenly frantic. He strode to the piano and with not a second's thought wrenched Cherry's stool from beneath her. She shrieked and thudded on the floor, arms and legs everywhere, her hat like a halo a yard away, astonishment all over her wide-open face—wide-open eyes, wide-open mouth—and made choking sounds that didn't frighten Shane in the least. 'So *there*,' he said to her, 'so blooming *there*!'

'Hey,' Normie was saying, 'hey, hey.'

And Leah, aghast, was watching the door, certain that it was the moment for Auntie Sadie to walk in, but Auntie Sadie didn't. Nobody walked in. It was Shane who walked out. He turned in the doorway and looked back. 'You awful lot of creeps. If you want to get into trouble, get into it, *on your own*!'

'Shane!'

He heard Normie's protest, but didn't answer it. He jumped the steps at a single bound, hit the path hard, then ran.

That flat Main Street where Auntie Sadie cried was so absurdly narrow; tens of thousands of empty square miles and a paved crown so narrow that two cars in modern times could scarcely pass abreast without raising a cloud of dust from the edges, and the driver who wanted to turn had to complete the manoeuvre by edging back and forth. Company land in the first place of course; they had always been a tight-fisted lot.

Everything was so crowded, so compact, so cluttered; stupid little blocks of land, except for two or three, houses only a few yards from the street, everybody in the old days living in everybody else's pockets. Only one decent house left standing. Her own. Dead centre at the top of town, commanding the scene, like an overseer's eye, around which even the road had to skirt.

She walked up the middle, going nowhere, tears on her cheeks. Had anyone ever seen her cry? Never. Except (at this moment) Peter, Cherry's little brother, only six. He walked beside her, looking up. 'Don't cry, Auntie Stevenson.'

Trees almost overhanging, all introduced, all brought in as saplings eighty years ago from hundreds of miles away, now half-rotten in the girth, riddled with fat white grubs and wasps, breaking bough by bough dangerously in high winds, cracking on frosty nights with sounds like gun-shots, waking children with a start.

'Don't cry, Auntie Stevenson.'

Empty shops with sagging verandahs and blistered forgotten names, grey weatherboard walls sun-bleached, gasping for paint or eaten out by termites until only shapes were left, as soft as cardboard through which a boy's fist could punch a hole. The old Bank of New South Wales, a burnt-down heap. Fences with scarcely a picket in place. Almost everything combustible taken away for fuel until even scavenging children felt stabs of conscience and now waited for standing things to fall before carrying them off.

'I'll kiss it better, Auntie Stevenson; let me, please, if it hurts.'

The telephone box outside Elliot's Store, bright red, looking ridiculous, newly painted last week by P.M.G. men who came in a truck and stayed overnight in a spare room available for travellers at the back of the shop. Bill Elliot couldn't sell his business and move away because no one would buy it without a proper lease and too few people owed him too much, and perhaps, like others, he feared the competition of big town life. No one with any spirit was left. The Police Station unoccupied for thirty years. The Anglican Church a heap of rubble pulled down with chains and tractors in 1946 because it was unsafe.

(How she had wept.) This house abandoned. That one a wreck.

'Why should I care?' she said aloud, 'does anybody else? It's not worth the heartbreak.'

'I care, Auntie Stevenson. I'll kiss it better.' Peter took her hand and tugged demandingly. 'Auntie Stevenson! I *care*! Why don't you look?'

She found him there, to her faint surprise. 'Hullo, dear,' she said. 'Care? About what?'

'I care that it hurts, Auntie Stevenson.'

'What hurts you, Peter?' Her smile was vacant. Her eyes seemed to be looking somewhere else.

'Not me, Auntie Stevenson; you. I'll kiss it better.'

'Will you, Peter?' She squeezed his hand but it was an unfeeling response. 'Run along, dear. I have a phone call to make.'

'You've passed the phone box. It's way back there.'

'Have I? Well, aren't I an old silly? It's just as well I have you here to put me right.'

'Who are you going to ring up, Auntie Stevenson?'

'I don't know, Peter. I'll think of someone.'

He started pulling on her, taking her back. She wanted to dab at her face, but couldn't, somehow, while he was looking on, flushed face upturned, big eyes with a little boy's question mark.

'Why are you crying, Auntie Stevenson?'

'I'm not, dear. Really I'm not. Old ladies' eyes water sometimes, that's all.'

He brought her to the telephone box. 'Why aren't you in Sunday School? Why are you walking up the street? Haven't you got a hanky to wipe your eyes?'

'Yes, I have a hanky.' But she had left her handbag in the hall. 'Oh, dear,' she said, and instinctively patted at her cheeks.

'You can have mine,' he said, and produced for her a tiny cotton square with red kittens and chewing-gum on it.

'No, thank you, dear. I'm all right. Run along. Mummy will be wondering why you're not home. She won't let you come to Sunday School next week if you don't go straight home this week to change your clothes. And I wouldn't like that at all. I don't know what I'd do if you weren't there.'

He weighed the statement gravely, because she had introduced a serious matter. 'Promise not to cry any more, Auntie Stevenson.'

'I promise, dear.'

Then he ran and she stepped stiffly into the stifling shade of the store verandah and sat on the hard box seat under a window full of pots and pans and tins of soup with faded labels.

'I must go back to those children,' she said aloud. But couldn't. She couldn't even ring up. Her small change was in her handbag foolishly left in the hall. Perhaps it was for the best. If she had spoken her mind to Mr. Garrett, exactly as she felt, she might have brought a judgment on herself, if God knew of course, if He cared as much as a little boy of six.

'Mr Garrett,' she said, but only to herself, 'I give not a tinker's curse for your precious slips of paper. If you wave them under my nose one more time I'll tear them up. Since when has any man owned the earth except when his bones are dust? I don't care if your slips of paper are supposed to give you the right to every speck of dirt. You don't own me, Mr Garrett. You don't own that little boy of six. You'll push this town off the map over my blood and flesh. You don't scare me even if you scare the rest. I'll fight. I've lived my life in Chinaman's Reef. I'll not be driven out to die anywhere else. That cemetery out there is my piece of earth. I want six feet of it. You'll not rob me of that.'

An old dog with his tongue hanging out, Labrador and fat, panted along the pavement and sat at her side. He thumped his tail to attract her attention and she fondled his well-bitten ear. 'And so say you, Jack,' she said, 'there are two of us, at least.' But it would have been more effective if she had brought the money to ring up. That was the stupid sort of thing she had done all her life.

'I've got to get back to those children.'

But the old dog put his head against her and his contentment was at that moment more important than anything else. They had meant too much to each other for too long. Then she cried again. She tried hard not to, but some things could not be held back, because she was not the fighting kind. She had never fought anything in her life except the weaknesses she had discovered in herself. She had always gone the extra mile to love people even when loving them was a torment or a feat of strength. She had always put herself last, always lived as she believed God wanted her to live, always endured all things without complaint.

'Shane!'

Normie bellowed into the heat across the open ground that began at the back of the hall and ended hundreds of miles off; grassland in spring and after rains, grassland and flowers, but now it was a shimmering wasteland of tussocks and scrub defoliated by goats and sheep, with rusted poppet-heads and pale chimney stacks standing where fortunes had been won, and evil green heaps of slag, and a railway track, straight as a line of sight, that hadn't heard a train whistle since 1923.

There was no sign of Shane, but he could have dropped out of view, dropped into a depression or plunged into the scrub. Shane could move. Over short distances he was like a greyhound on his feet.

'Shane,' yelled Cherry. 'Look, I'm sorry. True I am. It was my fault. I'll play *Onward Christian Soldiers* if you want me to.'

But Shane didn't answer and they couldn't make too much fuss because their voices might carry back to town and then all hell would break loose.

'The silly coot,' grumbled Normie, 'now what'll we tell her when she comes back? Crazy thing to do. *Shane!* For Pete's sake!'

'He shouldn't have taken it so seriously,' Cherry said. 'Shane's not like that.'

'Well he's like it this time, but you did stick the boots in a bit.'

'I didn't mean to. Shane knows I didn't mean it. Golly, Normie, we don't fight.'

'How did it happen?' wailed Leah. 'I mean, just like that. What's Auntie Sadie going to say? She'll be so upset.'

'*Shane*,' bellowed Normie, then waved an arm. 'Where do you look? Where do you start? Strike me, once he's out there you'd need a hundred blokes to run him to earth, if the bloomin' snakes don't get him first.'

'He's stupid,' Cherry said, 'and who's the one that's sore,

anyway? Me. I'm the one that got thumped.' She pulled a wry face and rubbed the part that hurt. 'He shouldn't have done it, you know. It's dangerous. Girls have got to be careful with things like that.'

'If we go inside,' said Leah, 'do you think he'll come back?'

'Sure he will,' growled Normie, 'but when? Before Auntie Sadie or after? She'll start a riot, honest she will. Do you remember anythin' like it happenin' before? *Ever?*' The magnitude of the question overwhelmed him.

'How did it happen?' repeated Leah. 'I mean, just like that. A fight in Sunday School . . . *Shane*,' cried Leah with a terrible ache, 'do come back.'

'I've told him I'm sorry,' Cherry said, 'he must have heard. I can't do more than that. Like Leah says, if we go inside he might come back. I didn't think Shane was like that. Fair's fair, but this is a bit much. Anyway, where's Auntie Sadie? If she'd come back it wouldn't have happened.' Cherry was becoming cross. 'What'd she go away for like that?'

They returned to the front of the hall, half afraid they would find her there, waiting; but she wasn't.

'Talk about hide and seek,' moaned Normie, 'a real crummy morning this turns out to be.'

Leah was thinking partly of Shane and partly of her Bible reading, so carefully rehearsed, Psalm 49, twenty verses, hours getting the rhythm right. Cherry limped up the steps. 'I'm getting stiff,' she said, 'if that crumb has done me a damage!'

'Do you want me to look?' said Normie. 'I'll soon tell you.'

'You bally well won't, Normie Muir.'

'I don't mind,' Normie said.

'I'll bet you don't, you cheeky so-and-so.'

Leah didn't know where to hide herself. Her cheeks flamed so much that her eyes hurt. Frantically, she changed the subject. 'I think Auntie Sadie must be sick. Do you think we ought to check up? I mean, she was odd. It's not like her, going away. It's less like her, not coming back.'

'Yeh,' said Cherry, 'let's. With **Normie** here on his own I don't reckon us girls are safe.'

'Come off it,' said Normie, embarrassed.

You only had to run for a minute out of Chinanaman's Reef, taking any direction you liked, and you were on your own.

Shane lay among the tussocks, panting for a time, pulse pounding in his head. He was flat in the dirt, face down.

'Wouldn't it rip you. Wouldn't it just.'

He knew they were calling after him, but he was too ashamed to show himself, too confused at first to think. All he could do was feel.

'Shane!'

He had never had a row before, not a real one, with Cherry or Normie. You couldn't fight Cherry or Normie. It didn't happen. You were like one flesh.

'Shane!'

You belonged to each other. The first things of life you remembered were their faces and voices. The very idea of growing up and drifting apart could turn thought into pain. And it was beginning to happen, at least in him. Barriers were going up. There were blind spots where before there had been none. Their thoughts were going one way; his were going another.

'Gee.'

He rolled over a few times then lay on his back and closed his eyes to the brilliant sky. He could hear little kids yelling somewhere, he could hear magpies, he could hear goats bleating, he could hear Leah: 'Shane, do come back.'

But Leah was nothing.

He lay there with eyes closed to the sky, tall grass a wall of wire for hiding behind.

CHAPTER THREE

The Tearing Apart

AFTER a while they didn't call any more and Shane tried hard
not to think of Auntie Sadie but it was like trying not to breathe.
She'd be furious, she'd be hurt, and people didn't do things to
upset Auntie Sadie, not openly anyway, that she'd be likely to
find out.

Grandpa Baxter used to say that Auntie Sadie kept Chinaman's Reef alive. Just by being there on that hillock at the other
end of town, like someone presiding over the table, just by
showing herself walking down the street, just by being what she
was, she held the place together, the last few families. She kept
it civilized, by example. She was the only decent thing be-
queathed by the old mining company to Chinaman's Reef.
There'd be nothing left for anyone when Auntie Sadie died.
That was what Grandpa Baxter used to say when *he* had been
alive. Then everyone would go away and there'd be a ghost
town on the plains left to the rabbits and crows.

Winds wailing, broken doors ajar, gardens dead for want of
water, no kids, no piano from Cherry's house. Winds wailing
and silence.

Where would Shane be then?

He'd be in the future. What on earth was that? It'd be a city,
he supposed. Millions and millions of people all looking alike;
Normie and Cherry, too; they'd all look alike and he'd never
tell one from the other. They'd all be swallowed up, like almost
everyone born in Chinaman's Reef for years and years. They
all packed up, all went away, nearly all to Sydney or Melbourne
or Adelaide. He felt flat and empty and cold. They'd been
doing it for years because there was nowhere else to go.

It was like a wheel that had to turn, that couldn't help itself.
It was like the fight with Normie and Cherry. It had had to

come, if not today then at some other time. It was the beginning
of the tearing apart, the beginning of the going away. He was
older than they were, after all.

There were fellows in cities digging roads, carrying loads,
getting their hands real dirty to earn a living. Kids from
Chinaman's didn't rate for much more. They seemed to wear
a badge that city people could read. *Hick*, the badge said, *here's
another one ripe for cutting down.*

Kids from Chinaman's headed for cities like moths for the
fire and the cities singed them. They never turned into people
you heard about, just got swallowed up. Unless they played
football, like George McQueen, but he had left Chinaman's
when he was four.

The local fellows weren't polished; they were rough-hewn.
They weren't educated. School was too far away. Sure, you
went to school every schoolday, sat in the stinking hot bus and
jolted off to Kenyon, kids from miles around, kids from places
so far away you never knew whether they lived in houses
or huts or hollow trees. It was a long, long ride to Kenyon
Area School, and a long ride home. Riding so far made you
tired.

You thought you learned a lot, but you didn't. You thought
you were real bright, but you weren't. You thought you'd be
something in the world but you ended up pushing a shovel.
That's what Roger said last time he came home; it's what
Horrie Muir said when he came home; it's what Cherry's sisters
said in slightly different words; they all said the same.

They stopped a few days, swaggering a bit in their city
clothes, vowing never to go back there. 'Chinaman's is the
place,' they said, 'goats' milk, real homemade cheese. Fresh air,
here a body can breathe. There's no place like Chinaman's,'
and went fishing in the Devil's Kitchen and kangaroo shooting
on the plain. But when they went to look up their old mates
they'd all gone away. On Saturday nights there was nothing to
do. There wasn't a pub, they said, and a dance only twice a
year. Not even TV unless you spent a fortune sticking your
aerial half a mile in the sky and didn't mind if your screen
looked like snow. 'How do you stand the dump?' they said. 'It
gets worse every year. When you come to town, kid, look me up.

I'll introduce you to a bloke who can use a young fellow with muscle up his sleeve.'

That might have been all right for Normie, but not for Shane. He was too light, too small, and heavy physical effort *hurt* him somehow; it was not pain, just a hurt, as if the strength he called upon was meant to be used another way. He didn't want to spend his life digging trenches and making roads. That's all a fellow did whether he stopped at home or went away. That was all that any of their fathers did, looked after roads that hardly anyone used. Except Leah's dad, who 'starved to death' keeping the store. 'Stop worrying about it,' Mum used to say, 'you're young yet. I've never known a boy to get in such a state over things that are years ahead. It'll be all right when the time comes. If you don't want to swing a pick, do something else, but it's honest labour and honest pay. There are factories. Perhaps you can work in a garage. There are shops. You're good at figures, after all.' They were used to the idea that the grown-up boys and girls would live in cities, in boarding-houses and hostels, would come home once or twice, then disappear. You found them only when you went looking for them; it rarely worked the other way.

He felt sick and sat up in the tussocks to shake the feeling off. His head swam a little; it was hot; it was stupid, he knew, lying there without shade of some kind. Farther west a couple of hundred miles or so, where the arid zone began, they said you'd die in nine hours, dehydrated, if you couldn't find water or shade.

But there was more to his feeling than that. It was strange. There was an uneasiness as if the sickness were more of the ground than of himself. He put his hand to it, carefully, bearing gently down, but there was nothing unusual, of course. The ground was the only thing that never changed. If you went away it was always there. If you came back in a year it still was there. Even if you never came back it didn't budge an inch.

He put his ear to it, deliberately, with a sense of drama, pressing hard with the side of his head, and in a while sat up, puzzled.

Something was wrong in the earth.

There was a murmur down there, extremely faint, very deep.

He scanned the pale sky, that vast blazing sky, and a little unsteadily found his feet, almost afraid that the earth would begin to quake.

A long way off, at ten miles or so perhaps (you could never tell for sure), he saw a granular cloud lying low over the plain, separate from it, as if stretched out for a rest on a cushion of shimmer.

CHAPTER FOUR

House-Cleaning

PETER COOPER, only six, said to his mother, 'Auntie Stevenson hasn't got a clean hanky to wipe her tears. Can I take her a hanky when I've changed my clothes?'

Mrs Cooper, not greatly concerned, went to her gate to check up and peered back along the street. 'Of course she's not there. Tears? Sadie Stevenson? What will that child come home with next?' But a detail had escaped her. In part at least the boy was right. A woman in black sheltered in the shade of Elliot's Store.

'Crying? I don't believe it.' But it was an extraordinary thing for the child to have said. 'What's the old dear doing there, anyway? Why isn't she with the children? Sunday School's not over. It's nowhere near eleven-thirty.' She called back through the house to her husband. '*Owen!* Can you hear me? Will you come outside?'

Normie, still looking sheepish, trailed Cherry and Leah into the street from the other end. You never knew where you were with girls. Cherry was terrific but went all peculiar at times. He'd only been having fun. They were treating him like a disease. 'Do you think we'd better go to her house?' Leah said. 'I can't see her anywhere, can you?'

Normie grumbled. 'Pigs to everyone. I'm goin' home. What's the use?'

'There's someone near the phone box,' Cherry said, 'could that be her?'

'Sure,' scoffed Normie, 'playin' hopscotch with the little kids. Look at her jumping up and down.'

'Under the verandah, stupid! Rub the dust out of your eyes; Sitting on the seat!'

Normie squinted into the glare. 'Crikey, she is, you know. She's on the seat, all huddled up.'

Stan Baxter, father of Shane, in soiled shorts and singlet, wheeled a barrow across the road with a gift of cleanings from his poultry shed for the Muirs' lettuce bed. He saw the children running and the Coopers hurrying from their gate. 'What's up?' he thought, 'don't tell me someone's struck it rich!' He put his barrow down and called, 'Hey, Owen. What's the lark?'

Bill Elliot, father of Leah, stepping into the store from his residence at the rear, took a packet of tea from the shelf and saw the old lady's back propped awkwardly against the window glass. It gave him quite a shock. Beyond her in the glare the Coopers were poised like a photograph, as if they had been running and had been snapped at the instant of having stopped.

Cherry sobbed and hobbled along behind (that blooming Shane) wincing from her aches, not used to seeing Leah out in front. She wanted to run but a wild and awful thought was making her weak. 'Tell me she's not dead. Gee, she just couldn't be that.'

Of these things Auntie Sadie was in a way aware. They were happening in a world remote from herself, but registered, oddly, through her dog. He was her eyes and voice, and he growled with an unusually threatening note.

'Miss Stevenson!'

They were indistinct, like faces seen through curtains of water. A hand reached out, but dropped; the dog was uneasy and sounded dangerous. He had been very irritable of late. 'Don't be silly, Jack,' she said, but no one heard her, only saw the movement of her lips.

'What's wrong with her?' It was Normie sounding breathless. 'She went away and didn't come back. We waited and waited.'

'Oh, Auntie Sadie, are you sick?' Leah was forgetting herself because they never called her by that name face to face.

The shop door opened and Leah's parents came out, Mrs Elliot fluttering a little, bird-like. Cherry hobbled up, crying with relief. Sick people got better; she didn't mind so much if Auntie Sadie was only sick.

The dog growled continually, holding everyone back. He was old and fat but he was a black Labrador and not to be trifled with. 'Don't be silly, Jack,' she said, 'we're all friends here, you know that,' and slipped one hand through his collar and the other about his neck.

'I'll get you a cup of tea,' Leah's mother said, hoping to escape. Illness made her nervous. 'It won't take a minute.'

Auntie Sadie shook her head.

'Really, I insist.'

Her husband restrained her. 'No, if she doesn't want it.'

Mrs Cooper said, 'Why are you like this? Goodness me, you gave us a fright.'

But she couldn't see any of them clearly and didn't want them crowding about. She dropped her head and tears fell into her lap. 'Please go away. I'm all right. I want to be by myself. I'm just a little upset.'

But they didn't go away and the eyes of the adults were turning to the children.

'What have you lot been up to?'

'Nothing, Mum,' Cherry shrilled, 'nothing at all.'

'Yeh,' grumbled Normie. 'Why blame us?'

'We didn't do anything,' Cherry went on, 'honest we didn't. She must have had bad news or something.'

'What? Bad news in Sunday School?'

'She came out to meet us like she always does, then walked away.' Leah looked from face to face, horrified that anyone might imagine an unruly act of which she could have been a part. 'True, true; we didn't do anything, Mrs Cooper. We didn't, Mr Baxter; you don't have to look like that. She put Shane in charge and went away.'

'Where's Shane then?' he asked, 'where is he? And young Garrett? Once *he* gets off the chain he's the worst of the lot.'

'The Garretts didn't come,' said Normie, 'and Shane's still back there . . . cleaning up . . .' It was a stupid thing to say, but he couldn't think of anything else soon enough.

'Cleaning up what?'

Normie was beaten for the moment and hoped desperately for support, but Leah and Cherry looked as blank as he felt. 'I—don't know,' he stammered. 'He just didn't come.'

'Why not?' Shane's father's questions had the weight of a threat. 'What's he cleaning up? Either he's cleaning something up or he's not. What's he broken? What's he been and done?'

'It's mischief all right,' Mrs Cooper agreed, 'you kids have been up to something. You're so dirty, Cherry. Just look at you, for heaven's sake. Dirt all over your dress. And where's your hat?'

Auntie Sadie looked sharply up, with anger rising unexpectedly. 'It has nothing to do with the children! They have not misbehaved! For goodness' sake leave them alone.' She felt irrationally angry, disconcerting even herself. 'Has it ever occurred to you people that I'm human like any other one of you? That I can become distressed for *private* reasons.' Then she turned on Shane's father with intense irritation. 'For pity's sake do not stand upwind of me. You stink to high heaven.'

'Uh?' he said, aghast.

'I have hinted so often, Stan Baxter, and to your father before you, to deep litter your fowls. There should not be a smell like that. You're a public nuisance. When the town goes at least your loathsome fowl house will go with it. There! It's said. I've been going to say it for years. At last it's said.'

She lurched to her feet, forgetting the dog, almost strangling the poor brute until she released him and he dropped coughing at her feet. Hurting her dog, because of them, incensed her further and her voice rose in pitch. She didn't want to stop, didn't want to hold anything back, suddenly didn't care who she hurt. Flesh and blood could stand only so much. 'Let's have a house-cleaning before I burst.' She snapped her teeth. 'Leah, if you don't take your finger out of your mouth I think I'll scream. If there's one thing I cannot abide it's finger-nails chewed down to the quick.' She waved angrily at the store. 'And tell your father to remove those horrid soup tins from the window of his shop. They're enough to put you off food for life.' Her dull eyes almost flashed at Cherry's father. 'Owen Cooper, you've got to drink a lot less or buy a larger pair of pants; your bulging belly makes me sick—and you were such a sweet little boy. Normie, part your hair on the side and fluff it up. Don't slick it down and comb it back. You look like—Lord, save us, I don't know what. Cherry, if you mince your hips one more time like a cheap little hussy I think I'll go berserk.'

She stomped on to the street.

'Chinaman's Reef! A lifetime I've stomached it and for what? Fight for it? What is there to fight for?'

Then there was nothing except horror in her, except astonishment at herself, and her anger drained out and she seemed to shrink.

They said not a word; they were stunned beyond belief. Leah's hand fell to her side and she turned away her head. Cherry's father, unusually pale for a man of florid face, wished for the earth to open up.

Auntie Sadie stood limply, almost dying of shame and regret, stood there shrinking, draining out. 'I'm sorry,' she suddenly cried. 'Oh, dear friends, I'm sorry, forgive me if you can; it's only because I love you and so little time is left.'

They didn't understand. They remained stunned, as if she had taken to them with a switch. Never in the memory of anyone, old or young, had she criticized, had she judged, had she ever uttered a word that had been directed to hurt.

She looked from one to the other, cruelly reproaching herself for having told nothing but the truth, then Mr Elliot took his wife by the arm and went back into the shop. 'Leah,' he called from inside, 'you're wanted,' and Leah, hiding her hands, trying not to cry, followed her parents, groping over the step.

'Come along,' said Mrs Cooper, first to her husband, then to Cherry, 'that certainly clears the air a bit. Tuck your stomach in, Owen, in case you trip. Watch your hips, Cherry. Try walking on your head.'

'I'm sorry,' Auntie Sadie cried. 'Oh, Rose, have a heart.'

'Yeh,' said Shane's father, 'give her a break. She did her block, so what? You know what it's like yourself. If these things upset her, well they do, that's that. And maybe she's right. I stink a treat.'

'Your problem, Stan Baxter,' said Mrs Cooper, with a toss of her chin, 'will wash off. Ours won't. Ours, apparently, are built in. As for you, Normie, do as you're told, get yourself home and scrub that grease off your scalp. You look like a racecourse tout. If you come knocking at our door again with hair like that I'll turf you out on your ear.'

Then, righteously indignant, she went a few steps but somehow lost her stride, seemed to hesitate, and stopped.

Her husband hadn't moved and Cherry felt frightened and sick. 'I'm coming, Mum,' she said, in a bewildered voice.

But Mrs Cooper didn't hear and was not aware that her family had been slow to march. She stood as though an obstacle no one else could see interrupted her path.

'It's perfectly true,' she said aloud, addressing herself, 'that shop window is a disgrace. You get so used to it you never expect anything else.' She looked back. 'Do you *mince* your hips, Cherry? It's something you must know about. Do you? If Miss Stevenson says so, then you must.'

Auntie Sadie, almost distraught, shook her head. 'No, no, of course she doesn't. I'm a silly old woman. Oh, Rose, let it drop.'

'Sure she minces 'em,' thought Normie rebelliously, 'and she looks terrific. Like my hair. It looks terrific, too. The old crab. I'll not be scrubbin' anythin' off.' He started edging away, getting ready to run.

'Cherry,' said her mother, 'I've not noticed it, but it's true. You do. And it's not very nice.' She shot a glance at her husband's stomach billowing over his belt and raised her eyebrows with a sniff. 'Love's blind, all right,' she said, 'how could I live with *that*? . . . I'm with you, Miss Stevenson; we'll let nothing drop.'

But something like anguish was on Auntie Sadie's face and Stan Baxter was getting nervous, sensing a fight. 'You heard what she said, Rosie girl. Enough's enough. It doesn't matter what I admit, that's my business. You're getting deliberate, Rose, that's different from doing your block.'

'For heaven's sake; what sort of talk is that?'

'It's common sense,' her husband said, tight-lipped. 'You're getting reckless, Rose. Next time you might find that it's yourself.'

Auntie Sadie shook her head again and again, but no power on earth could call her words back.

'Look,' Mrs Cooper complained, genuinely mixed up, 'I'm trying to make the peace, not break it.'

'I know, I know, my dear.' Auntie Sadie was in despair. 'But the damage is done. I'm sorry and I can't account for myself. If there ever was a point it's been lost. I've just got to be by myself. I think I want to go home . . .'

But she didn't move. She stood there, still draining out, waiting only for the children to forgive her, but doubting if they ever would. Children were not like grown-ups; their wounds cut deep. She couldn't say things to children that only parents had the right to express. Leah had gone and had not come back, Normie inch by inch was shuffling off, Shane? (where was Shane?), and Cherry was hurt. Did she really know she minced her hips? A warm-blooded creature like her might never have guessed, and was it a tragedy? If she couldn't help herself that was that. 'You silly old woman,' she accused herself, 'are you jealous because she's young?'

Then Normie went, a stumble became a stride and he was off, feeling completely out of his depth. Something serious had happened, but he didn't know what. 'Anyway, my Mum likes my hair,' he stammered, and ran, 'and the kids reckon it's beaut.'

'Normie, don't,' Cherry cried. 'She said she was sorry.'

But Normie ran one way and because of it Cherry had to run another. She knocked Auntie Sadie almost from her feet and threw her arms about her, more like a mother than a girl of fourteen. She hugged the trembling old body, probably something that had not happened in fifty years, panicking Auntie Sadie. 'Cherry, you mustn't . . .'

'I understand, Miss Stevenson, I do, I do.'

'Let me go, Cherry, please.'

'Oh, Miss Stevenson, I hate myself. I said the same sort of things to Shane. Shane's not cleaning up, he ran away.'

'Cherry, Cherry, you're hurting Miss Stevenson. For heaven's sake, child, release her.'

'What's this about Shane?' Stan Baxter barked. 'Shane running away?'

'Cherry!' Her mother took her firmly by the arms and broke her grasp. 'Darling,' she shouted, 'you're *hurting* Miss Stevenson. Don't you understand?'

Cherry sobbed and dropped her head. 'I was hurting her more before.'

'That's not the point; you mustn't manhandle people like that.'

Auntie Sadie was gasping for breath. 'Oh my goodness.'

'What's this about Shane?' persisted Stan Baxter. 'I thought someone said there hadn't been trouble; or am I completely nuts?'

'That was *after*,' wailed Cherry, 'not before.'

Mrs Elliot stuck her nose out of the shop and hastily drew it back.

'Normie,' Stan Baxter bellowed, 'come here! What's this about Shane?'

But Normie was long out of sight. 'I'll get him,' Mr Cooper said, 'but kids run off you know, Stan, at the drop of a hat. It's probably nothing much.'

'Maybe not. But something's at the bottom of it. We've had our noses pushed off the scent. What's this about the town? About my fowl house and all that? Why's there not much time left?'

Owen Cooper, a dozen paces up the street, looked back. 'That's a point. What *is* at the bottom of this?'

'I want to know where Shane fits in. What's this about Chinaman's, Miss Stevenson, and stomaching it and for what?'

The background was filling. The small fry were coming out, like rabbits out of holes, but standing back, wary of what looked like a stand-up fight between grown-ups. Bill Elliot, in a temper, was leaning into his window, knocking saucepans and display cans right and left. Mr and Mrs Albert Muir, on the warpath, came out through their front gate propelling Normie an arm's length in front. Auntie Sadie took Cherry by the shoulders and gave her a gentle squeeze. 'Thank you, dear,' and again choked up.

Shane came running, shouting at the top of his voice. 'Hey, everyone, hey, hey. Something's up!'

'For crying out loud,' Stan Baxter yelled at his son, 'where have you been?'—and spotted his wife with a towel over her shoulders and her hair full of froth.

Albert Muir's voice came rolling down the street, 'Is it bush week or what?'

Shane arrived, hot and panting, drenched in sweat.

'Look here, young fellow, what the devil's been going on?'

Owen Cooper yelled back, 'Keep your hair on, Albert.'

'There's a dirty great cloud of dust,' Shane panted, 'only a few miles off.'

Mrs Muir added shrilly to the din, 'I reckon it's a crummy sort of thing to say to a kid.'

'Please, Mum,' wailed Normie, 'forget it, will you.'

Shane's mother padded up in dressing-gown and slippers, trying to blow froth off her face, trying to see through a lather of soap.

'Honest injun,' Shane panted, 'I don't know what it is. I reckon you'd better come and look. It's something for sure. Something's up.'

Mrs Elliot again poked her head out of the shop, with darting eyes, more than ever like a bird.

'Who's struck it rich?' Shane's mother said. 'Has someone won the State lottery?'

'Honestly,' cried Mrs Cooper, waving her arms.

'What do you mean—a cloud of dust? What do you mean—something's up?'

'Look for yourself, Dad. You'd better come. Say, Normie, you'd better be in on this.'

'Great grief; what's the smell? Stan Baxter, have you been in that fowl house again?'

'Strike me dead, woman. Don't *you* start.'

'Are we to get an apology?' demanded Mrs Muir. 'You threaten to turf my son out on his ear. You and who else? What's wrong with his hair, I ask you? I can believe it of you, Rose, but Miss *Stevenson*?'

'I stand by my wife. I don't go for that kind of talk. Don't threaten me, Owen. Don't you raise your voice to me.'

'Threaten you? I haven't opened my mouth.'

'If it's a punch on the nose you want, mate, you've come to the right address.'

'So help me bob, I didn't open my mouth, I haven't said a word.'

'It looks like the army coming again, Dad, fair dinkum it does. Isn't anyone going to look? Hey, what's everybody fighting about? Hey, Normie. Hey, Cherry. What's going on?'

'*Will you all shut up!*' Shane's father bellowed, then rammed his hand into his ribs and doubled over. 'Strike me dead, I think I've collapsed me lungs.' He looked up with an agonized face, and for the moment at least was the centre of attention.

'Look,' he pleaded, 'we're carrying on like a lot of nuts. Shane's trying to tell us something. The kid's seen something. Tell 'em, Shane.'

'Gee, Dad, are you all right?'

'Yeh, yeh. I'll live. It's happened before. Get on with what you've got to say. Say it.'

'What are you all fighting for? Golly, you ought to hear yourselves?'

'Not *that*. Just tell us what you've seen.'

'Dust—like I said. A dirty great cloud of dust. I don't know what it is. It's shaking the earth.'

'The earth shaking? What are you talking about? The earth's not shaking.'

Shane pointed beyond the Pride of Ballydoon and the blacksmith's shop and the hall. 'That's where it is, out there, on the plain. Honest injun, I'm not fooling, something's coming this way, for sure.'

Auntie Sadie caught her breath, so sharply that everyone heard. 'Not today. Not on a Sunday.' From the look of her Shane had hit the spot.

Normie's father bristled. 'Is somebody having us on? Who are the donkeys round here? Us?'

Stan Baxter set off with a deliberate step. 'All right, son. Show me.'

'What is it, Shane?' Normie yelled.

'I don't know. Come and look. Hey, Cherry, coming with us?'

Cherry was wanting to, badly, to get away from the storm and tempest, but her father took a light hold on the old lady's arm, with respect, and called down the street, 'This is where we'll find out. Right here, I reckon.'

They were usually very polite when she was about but Shane's father called impatiently, 'Well, come on. What is it? How much longer are we going to mess about?'

But Auntie Sadie was not to be rushed. She had gone through too much.

'What is it, dear? Mrs Cooper said. 'Aren't you going to tell us? Is this what the morning's been about?'

'Yes,' Auntie Sadie sighed. 'But it couldn't happen *today*.'

'Well if it couldn't happen,' growled Albert Muir, 'whatever it is, what are we worried about? Let's settle the argument and get some peace.'

Cherry's father was showing fresh signs of irritation. 'What couldn't happen, Miss Stevenson?'

'The open cut!'

'What open cut?' He dropped her arm. 'What are you talking about?' (Was the old dear completely off her rocker?)

'He always threatened he would. Always said he would. That's why he bought everybody up. You've been deceived. He owns everybody and everything.'

'Who does?' Stan Baxter came pacing back. 'Who owns what? You don't mean Garrett?'

'Garrett,' sniffed Normie's father.

'Yes, I mean Mr Garrett. He said he would as soon as the price was right.'

'Said he'd do what?'

'Sell out.'

'I guess it's always been on the cards, Miss Stevenson, and it's nothing to get upset about.' Cherry's father was nonplussed, and was glancing particularly to big Albert. Albert Muir was boss. 'So he sells out. If he sells out someone buys. That's not going to worry us much. We get a new landlord, don't we, Albert? So what? It can't be worse than before; we might be a darn sight better off.'

'Come on, Dad. Aren't we going to look? Golly, I come rushing back here—'

'Quiet, Shane.'

Auntie Sadie was obviously close to tears again, to everyone's embarrassment, and they were not sure what to do with her. Weepy old ladies were difficult to deal with, particularly in the middle of the street. 'You're not understanding. It's different from that. It's not that he's sold out—it's a sell-out. I'm sure that's what they call it. Don't you understand? A *sell-out* . . . to the Pan Pacific Corporation.'

'Did I hear her right?'

Normie's father shouted, 'That's the best news ever. Stone me, woman, what's that to complain about?'

'Pan Pacific? It's the old Company. Well it is, isn't it? Why doesn't someone tell us these things?'

'They'll reopen the field. Well, it figures. It's not that it was really worked out.'

The small fry were galloping in, confident at last. The Elliots had come back to the edge of the crowd, Leah's father with a notably interested expression, but Auntie Sadie's head was down, her shoulders were bowed, and the noise they made was a load she had to carry. So many people. So much noise.

'Come on, Dad,' yelled Shane. 'That's who's coming. It must be Pan Pacific.'

There was an explosion in Shane's mind. The company would set up offices. There'd be jobs a fellow could do. He wouldn't have to go away and perhaps there were other fellows who could come back home. There might have been mothers and fathers who thought the same.

Auntie Sadie looked up. They'd never hear her now. They were on their way, streaming off to the end of town, impatient as always, never hearing anything out. 'You don't understand.' But her voice wasn't like a man's; it seemed to fall, unheard, at her feet.

They had gone, young and old, like a picnic crowd. It was the story of her life; people going away to goodness knows what without looking back, leaving her behind.

She turned the other way with her dog at her heels. In that direction was the hillock with a house on it, like a wart on a witch's nose.

But there wouldn't be a fight; if Pan Pacific were coming Garrett had beaten Chinaman's Reef hands down. How could you fight when the battle was lost before you had begun to prepare and the enemy was in your camp weeks before he was expected to appear? She had seen the Garrett children on Friday evening on the school bus passing through. He must have spirited them away, sent them off with his wife, betraying not only Chinaman's Reef but his family as well. They were children of the plains. How could they be happy anywhere else? Why did men forget so soon the things of the earth that children loved?

How could the Baxters and the Coopers and the rest, simple people who believed a man's word, grasp in minutes or seconds that Ronnie's father was not land-hungry in an ordinary way?

They had thought he was a mild sort of fool, with more money than brains, with an obsession to own a town. They had called themselves the realists and they had called him the fool. Buying up the leaseholds, one by one, the occupied places and the ones falling down, until nothing was left. Doing it in secret, keeping the facts from her. Turning leaseholders into tenants who thought they were secure for the rest of their lives. Exchanging their precious slips of paper for obvious material things like towering television antennae and washing-machines and 32-volt generators. 'We've still got roofs over our heads,' they said, 'for a few dollars a week and a lot more than we had before.' Would they ever believe that he had not been spending his own money, that he was not a sheep-man with a lust for land but a front for a syndicate of patient men who wanted the town and nothing more? The rest they already owned; they owned even her.

How could you stop Pan Pacific when it was *there*? Only a mile or two out of town. She had stood up to Garrett for years, coolly, wisely, even ruthlessly, to the last letter of the law, but the years had made her old. When it came to the showdown she was not the heroine stirring them to fight with well prepared words; she was the weepy old woman who didn't know what to do and had to go home.

CHAPTER FIVE

View from Chinaman's Slag

SHANE felt marvellously important and led the march jealously,
looking back over his shoulder to make sure that everybody was
still there. For the first time in his life, that he could recall, he
had achieved notoriety not only once but twice on the same
day, the second time better than before. Nothing back there
tickled his fancy as much as his own mother vigorously towelling
at the soap in her hair and trying to keep her slippers on and
her dressing-gown done up, shuffling after him, giving him a
quick smile. 'Gee, Mum,' he almost said, 'first I was in charge
of Sunday School and now I'm leading the town.' But he held
it back a little uneasily. He was going on fifteen, not a crummy
kid any more, and they were flimsy achievements after all.

Two or three of the small fry had a tendency to get out in
front and he did not approve. 'Get back,' he threatened silently,
with a penetrating scowl, 'or else!' But he had to walk faster and
faster, swinging his arms hard, until even Normie was struggling
to make the pace without breaking into a trot. 'What do you
reckon it is, Shane?'

'Like a blooming great storm.'

'Pan Pacific,' someone was saying, 'this I gotta see to believe.'

'We'll show 'em, eh?' Normie squeaked in the little-boy voice
that came out when he was excited. 'But fancy Auntie Sadie
knowing and not telling us an' all. She acted real funny, the
old crab.'

Shane shot him a puzzled glance.

'Criticizin' my hair.'

'Garrett's a bit of a clam,' grumped Bill Elliot from the rear,
'he could have given us some warning. If things are to happen
round here it wouldn't have hurt him, would it? I mean, I
could have stocked up the store. Well, it's for his good as well as

mine. Well it is, isn't it? A few paying customers for a change!'

'It's automation these days. They might do it with a couple of men and a can of oil.'

'Look, they've got to eat, haven't they? They've got to buy up somewhere. I can't see them driving to Kenyon, can you?'

'*She* wasn't too happy about it.'

'She's old. She's had it. You don't want to take any notice of her.'

'Something was on her mind, mate, and what are we good for, anyway, barring you, excepting cleaning out culverts and mending dirt roads?'

Normie bustled alongside. 'D'you reckon they could be workin' out there, Shane? Diggin' and all? Those geologists, you know, that have been hanging around. They could have started up without letting anyone know.'

'And us not seeing them from the bus coming home from school? Hey, Cherry. Did you hear this Normie Muir? Hey, where's Cherry?'

'You hurt her, you know, when you pulled out the chair.'

'Of course I didn't hurt her. What'd you call Auntie Sadie an old crab for?'

'Criticizin' my hair.'

Cherry lagged behind, aching like mad. Even her mother didn't realize she was not up with the crowd. 'He's done me a damage all right,' she gasped. 'I'll murder that Shane.' She limped into the shade of the Pride of Ballydoon to rest for a while and was surprised to find that the street was empty; she had expected Auntie Sadie to be back there. Only Leah was in sight, holding to a verandah post outside the store. Poor old Leah. Funny she had never noticed that Leah chewed her nails. But, golly, was it a sin and who cared? Cherry waggled her hips defiantly, even though it hurt, and immediately felt bad about it. She had forgiven Auntie Sadie and was not going to do it any more, but who would have imagined that such things could be said? Surely the mines opening up couldn't start off such a thundering row? Then she squinted the other way and the crowd had gone and following them was not important, not with Leah up there looking so much alone, and herself feeling so sore. After all, no one else in town was old

enough to be a friend or young enough to know what it was like
to be a teenage girl.

'There!' Shane yelled. 'See! I told you so!'

An enormous cloud-like formation, two miles or more wide,
looked in the brilliant sky like the threat of an approaching
storm, with numerous showers apparently pouring from it to the
ground. But that was not the way of it. It was the other way
about.

'It's closer than before,' Shane shrilled. 'They've turned in
from the highway for sure.'

It could have been taken for smoke if there had been anything of significance to burn. Scrub fires had been known in
that part of the world. It could have been taken for locomotives
in line astern consuming vast volumes of coal, except that the
cloud was red, not black, and there wasn't a railway line in
service closer than forty miles, and all the coal-burners had
been converted to oil or scrapped.

'Dust,' bellowed Albert Muir. 'Look at my road. It's blowing
away.'

There was an unmistakable sense of purpose in the cloud. It
knew why it was there and confidently possessed the right.

'My road,' roared Albert Muir, 'the blithering nerve. Tearing my road to pieces. What have they got on it, for cryin' out
loud?'

'If you don't know, Albert, how can we? They must have
told you heavy traffic was coming through.'

'*Must* have told me! What do you mean, *must* have told me?
I'm only the foreman round here. Nobody'll tell me the time of
day. On a Sunday. On a blitherin' Sunday! Can't even get the
water-cart out there to damp it down. I'll kill that Shire
Engineer.'

'You can't blame him, mate.'

'Can't I just? They can't move big stuff into the district
without gettin' the nod from the Shire. The Engineer's just
gotta know. I'll kill the cow.'

Normie hissed in Shane's ear, 'I'll race you to Chinaman's
Slag. We'll see it better from there.'

The telephone was ringing on the wall in the Post Office corner of the shop, drawing Leah in from the verandah post that she had hugged as if it had been alive. The telephone had been demanding her attention for half a minute or more until by sheer persistence it made itself heard. Leah stumbled in through the disorganized maze of open sacks, assorted casks and sleeping cats that littered the floor. 'Hullo,' she said, in a flat voice, 'Chinaman's Reef General Store.'

'Is that you, Madge?'

'No, it's Leah. Mum's not in just now.'

'Is your father there?'

'No.'

It was that horrible Miss Clapp from the Kenyon Exchange, thirty-eight miles away. Miss Clapp (in Mum's words) was an excellent reason for not answering the telephone.

'Can you get them for me, Leah? Can you bring them to the phone?'

'I don't think so, Miss Clapp. I think they've gone too far.'

'What's wrong, child?'

'Nothing.'

'Well, aren't you just jumping out of your skin for joy! You've heard the news, I suppose.'

'What news?'

'About Chinaman's Reef. You're famous out there.'

'Pardon?' said Leah.

'On the wireless. In the news. Don't your parents know? There's talk of turning you into an open cut.'

'What's an open cut?'

'Oh, Leah; you know, child. You couldn't be that ignorant. A great big hole. They're going to scoop you up and stick you through the crushers. Mangle, mangle. You know. An open cut.'

'They're going to what?' cried Leah.

'They're going to dig up the town.'

'*They can't do that!*'

'Oh yes, they can. I think you'd better get your father to the phone. Are you sure they don't know?'

Leah sickened and held the receiver an arm's length from her ear, then was compelled to drop it from her hand. It crashed against the wall and swung to and fro with broken chips of bakelite flaking to the floor.

'You horrible woman,' she screeched, 'you're everything they say you are. You horrible old crow.'

'Leah!' Cherry's silhouette shaded the open door and her call was a question of shocked surprise.

'Oh, Cherry, Cherry it's terrible. That horrible Miss Clapp says they're going to dig up the town. They're going to turn it into a *hole*.'

Normie thudded off towards Chinaman's Slag, running like a draught horse, as hard as he could go.

'Keep off that slag heap,' his mother shrilled. 'Don't you climb up there Normie, don't you dare.'

He could hear Shane's feet slapping close behind.

'Don't be silly, Leah,' Cherry squealed. 'You couldn't have got it right, and golly, look, you've broken the phone!'

'Blow the old phone. I've got to tell my Dad. He's got to stop them. He mustn't let them dig up the town.'

Something inside Cherry swelled like a tide. '*The open cut!* No one believed her. Auntie Sadie knew. Oh, Leah, that's why she was so strange.'

Normie's father suddenly raised an arm. 'Quiet. Quiet. Can't you hear? Will you kids shut down your noise.'

There was a rumble on the breeze, sounds like the tanks and troop carriers of half-forgotten battles fought long ago in deserts on the other side of the world. Goats were bleating. A vast flock of birds screeched and soared in a cloud of pink a mile away.

'Sounds like a war.'

'Dad! Dad! Dad!'

It was Leah in her white cotton frock running as no one had known she could.

'Oh, Dad! Dad!'

'Strike me array. What now?'

She leapt the ditch at the side of the road on to the open ground behind the hall, and three hundred yards away Shane and Normie staggered to the foot of the horrid-looking heap known as Chinaman's Slag, gasping for breath, stitches in their sides, not caring who won the race or how. There was a safe way up, if you took care, known to every man and boy who had ever felt the urge to stand like a king above the plain.

'Oh, Dad.'

Leah gasped against her father, burning up in the flush of her exertion, trying to frame words, with people oppressively about her, with women's cries of concern felt through the agitation of her mother's hands. Hands plucking at her dress and her father saying, 'What is it, Leah? Give her air. Of course she's not ill, Madge.'

'Oh, Dad. Miss Clapp on the phone. They're going to dig us up. They're going to turn us into a hole. It's been on the news. Oh, Dad, you mustn't let them.'

He pushed people aside and held her to him. She was panting against him, as hot as fire, her heart hammering. 'Give her air. Give her air.' He had known what she said, he had understood. Mr Elliot was no fool. 'Easy does it,' he said, more to himself than to Leah.

'It's true, Dad. I know it's true. It's what Auntie Sadie was trying to tell us. You should have heard that horrible Miss Clapp. Oh, Dad, I'm sorry, but I broke the phone. I couldn't stand her. I broke the phone.'

He was trying hard to delay the instant of total acceptance because beyond it was a place of absolute loss, of nothing, of going back to a new beginning that he was not young enough to face without fear.

Owen Cooper said, 'Godfathers. So that's the score.'

Shane's father had turned pale. 'It's the town. It's the town they want. The dirty dogs. Half a mile square and never worked. What the hell is underneath us down there?'

Normie's father could have spat. 'Not sand; you can bet your boots on that. And we don't own a foot of it. Garrett's got the lot. We're *tenants* in our own town!'

'Can we stake claims?'

'Who was that skirted galah?' Albert Muir glared at the

4

women, particularly at his wife. 'Claims? On Pan Pacific land? They'd eat you for breakfast.'

Leah wailed, 'What are we going to do?'

'Do?' Albert Muir snorted. 'We're *done*, like a dog's dinner.' He walked away a few paces beating at his mighty thigh with an enormous fist. 'My God, an open cut. But if the old dear knew, why didn't she tell us weeks ago? There must be *something* we could have done. Even we must have rights, God knows what, but there must be some.'

'Can't we stop them when they go through?'

'Grow up, woman! Who says they're going *through*!'

Cherry reached instinctively for the latch on Auntie Sadie's gate before she realized it wasn't there. The way was open. Never had she stepped through before without first unlatching the gate. Nobody ever left it open, because shutting it was the rule. It startled her like a stairway with a missing step or a book without a page and suddenly made her sensitive to many things she had noticed hardly ever, the love and labour that had formed a fussy garden of hundreds of bits and pieces on the knoll, pebbles and different sorts of stones and winding flagstone paths, flowers in bloom that no one else bothered to grow, bird baths and dovecots, three blue watering-cans in a line near the tap from the bore. Suddenly it made her want to cry. 'Oh, Auntie Sadie, it's such a shame.'

The house was open behind the screen door and gave off a breath of cool, old air. 'Miss Stevenson. Are you there?'

The silence beyond made Cherry aware of a rumble like a distant storm, a continuous rumble that rolled and rolled. She glanced back over the town and dust was clearly in the sky.

'Miss Stevenson!'

The old fat Labrador was somewhere in the hallway, wheezing; that was the only way she knew he was there. His blackness was lost in a mass of shadow lightened only by the brassy glimmer of a mirror.

'Don't you bite me, Jack,' she murmured, and opened the screen door against the grating and clicking of a long, narrow spring.

'Good boy, Jack. Don't bite. I won't hurt.'

Her eyes felt bruised from the sunlight outside and she made her way with care.

'Miss Stevenson, it's Cherry here.'

There was a room on her right, the blinds were down. In there, she knew, were old cedar chairs and a table with bulbous claws and an ornate green cloth with tassels hanging all around. There were sprays of pressed flowers in frames on the walls and an organ that squeaked when you pushed the pedals. Auntie Sadie was kneeling down.

'We *know*,' Cherry burst out. 'Oh, Miss Stevenson; what are we going to do?'

She ran to the old lady but suddenly had to pull her hands away. Auntie Sadie was saying prayers.

Normie reeled to the top of Chinaman's Slag seconds ahead of Shane. For a few moments he blinked into the glare, blood thudding in his temples, his throat dry and raw, his stitch not quite gone. He couldn't distinguish the sources of the cloud from the dust in the air, then his jaw dropped and he gaped open-mouthed. Shane began swaying beside him, panting, clutching at his side. 'Can you see it, Normie?'

'Yes . . .'

Shane could see nothing but stars, but when the stars went away, pinking out like tiny detonations in his head, he seemed to see with shocking clarity things that he knew were not there: armies, the flashing explosions of guns and of bombs, huge engines of war crushing the plain and discharging it as dust, faceless men in battle helmets marching in by the thousand and himself running away. But he was not running away, he was still clutching at the stitch in his side, hurting from it, and a long line of vehicles hundreds of yards apart, not clearly seen, obliterated the road as if the inheritance were theirs. Trucks and caravans and lorries, low-loaders with dozens of wheels, massed with machinery, drawn by diesels, red lights blinking through dust like points of fire, and a rumble that he could hear without even listening, engines of vast power, a clatter, a groaning. Every bird in miles was in the sky, animals were running,

Normie's voice sounded frightened. 'Gee . . . It's not anythin' like I imagined.'

Shane felt the thrust of a fierce resentment. They were invading his kingdom, callously overrunning something perfect. The silence and the stillness and the emptiness were being outraged by strangers without faces, by people glazed by windscreens.

'You can't come here,' he screeched, and shook his fist at them.

But they kept on coming.

They knew they were of no importance, they were little people and poor. They were only the road menders, their kids and wives, who lived way out back of beyond in a ghost town held together with bits of wire. Defiance was futile. Who but they cared?

'They can't.' Albert Muir banged his fist ineffectually into his thigh and walked a few paces more away, not only confused but ashamed. He was the foreman. On other days he said, 'We'll do this or we'll go there. We'll fill the potholes in B Section or take a run out to D and cut back the scrub.' Now he could give nothing to anyone but empty words. 'They can't. They can't.' But it was not a statement; it was the feeble cry of a helpless man.

The rumble grew and dust billowed from the earth where the tops of telegraph poles seemed to sink into the road.

Bill Elliot and his wife Madge hurried off to the store, to the phone. Shane's father and Cherry's father, understanding each other, started making their way with uncertainty to Chinaman's Slag, twice hesitating, once going on, but then turning back. What was the use of going up there when dust was bearing so close that at any moment vehicles must become visible from level ground? Young children fidgeted with something like excitement on the road, but it wasn't real excitement with laughter in it, it was an anxiety and a tenseness reflected from their parents. Albert Muir, entirely on his own, as if in a way he had accepted the blame, stood with hands on hips and face long-drawn staring blankly at the ground, wrestling with a brain that under pressure seemed incapable of functioning at all. The women were fidgeting, like the children, exchanging wry glances that they feared to hold for more than seconds at a time, overcome by an appalling sense of darkness and of emptiness, of not knowing anything any more, of even being surprised that they thought that way. It was like waking up in the morning in the cold to find yourself sleeping on stone, clothes gone, bed gone, house gone, town gone; alone in the world.

CHAPTER SIX

Chinaman's Belongs to Us

CHINAMAN'S SLAG was the throne and Shane was the king of a realm that no one but he cared was there, a universe of little things, abandoned by men, that helped to make up the boy.

'It's mine, not yours. You didn't want it any more.'

They must have been coming to the Slag, to the abandoned world on the flats below him, the left-overs of Chinaman's Reef Number 5, last and closest mine to town.

They'd take it back again. They'd turn in from the road on to the vanished track, crushing scrub and rabbit holes and a million wild flowers that would have burst through with the rains. They would overrun his world. They'd raze it to the ground and build it up again in a different way. Then they'd go down with enormous pumps prodigiously displacing the underground streams. They'd go down with machines chewing up rock and pulverizing bones.

He didn't want to work for them any more. You couldn't work for the destroyers of your world.

Men had died down there as far as seven hundred feet below on Easter Eve, 1919.

Oh, the stories that were told of that day.

The whistle blowing shrilly at the wrong hour, the sudden blast, the scream of steam that stopped dead the heart-beat of a town for unnumbered seconds of shock. Hundreds of doors suddenly opening, hundreds of people on the streets emptying out of houses through gates and over fences at the bound, out of hotels and schoolrooms and shops. Hundreds of people running one way along streets and across paddocks, bells ringing, the whistle's screaming in short and terrible bursts taken up like an echo by a shunting locomotive in the siding, awful sounds that people wished would stop. The Roman Catholic priest running from the altar in his vestments, the tragic collision of the Fire Brigade and Dr Henderson's car at the corner of Main Street and Ballydoon Lane, the Anglican bush brother riding in like a madman from eight miles out, his horse dying under him, hundreds of people running or riding or driving from every direction towards Chinaman's Reef No. 5. Almost all stopped hurrying before they got there. Death had a feeling and it travelled faster than people.

It was not gas or cave-in or fire.

Even now, for all that anyone knew, the old tunnels ranged about the central shaft like the roots of a tree drinking from deep artesian pools. Where the water rushed in from no one knew. They had never gone down again to find out why. There were murmurings of trouble of an ugly kind and the mine manager left town. Two weeks later he blew out his brains. They plugged the shaft and left Chinaman's Reef to die. Scores of wooden houses where streets used to be were jacked up, lowered on to drays, and carted away. It had happened long ago and for most the pain had gone.

A pale brown chimney stack was there rearing from the flats, still intact, left to boys and girls for making into dreams, a boy in one generation, a girl in the next, but now Shane. It had been a lighthouse beside angry seas, a building of fifty floors, the Tower of Babel for Auntie Sadie's tales, a rocket poised for flight to the moon.

Iron foundations were there set in crazed concrete yellow with dust and rust and age. Grass, as dry as splintered bone, clumped in the cracks. Huge old wheels were there, too heavy to roll away, from steam engines that had worked the stampers fifty years ago; monstrous wheels entangled in scrub and creeping vines that had been a hundred imagined things.

They were Shane's.

Brick piers and arches were there, like parts of ancient temples left behind by civilizations centuries extinct. Green stains and yellow stains and streaks of bronze fouled ground where nothing grew. Even now, sometimes, the air turned acrid when earth was disturbed.

Shane's great-grandfather had worked his last shift to a

sudden end at 2.19 p.m. on that almost forgotten afternoon, Easter Eve, 1919. Normie's great-grandfather, too.

Normie was pulling on Shane's arm. 'Are we going to let them?'

Shane couldn't bring himself back straight away, couldn't grasp that Normie was immediately real on the top of Chinaman's Slag, sharing with him something so intensely personal that it had seemed to be exclusively his own. 'Let them do what?'

'Whatever they're coming for? Auntie Sadie put on a terrible show. She doesn't want 'em, do you? She's scared and she's in the know. Are we going to stop them?'

There was a glimmer in Shane of where Normie's thoughts were going. Did he think he was a concrete wall? 'Stop that lot over there? Are you out of your mind?'

'Cut straight through. Cut 'em off at the road.'

'Cut them off? That lot over there? Do you think they'd stop for you? You're barmy.'

All Normie could foresee was himself on the road, dancing up and down, threatening Pan Pacific, holding them back by command. 'It's bad,' he said. 'I know it's bad. Auntie Sadie was in a terrible state, cryin' an' all.'

'I thought you were crook on her?'

'And so I am. But you know what she said, Ronnie's old man sellin' us out. And you can see it! It's stickin' out a mile.' Normie had to do something and had to do it hard, to set Ronnie Garrett's father back on his heels, to make Auntie Sadie feel bad, and to punch Pan Pacific clean between the eyes. 'Coming?' he said. 'I'm going to cut 'em off at the road.' He pointed over the one face of Chinaman's Slag that dropped sharply to ground level and put them closest to the road, that face quarried off and emptied back into the main shaft fifty years ago.

'Strike me,' Shane cried, 'not down there. Do you think you're Superman? Go the other way round.'

'By then they'll be gone. They'll be into town.'

'Normie,' Shane cried, 'no. Not from way up here. It's bad enough from half-way down.'

But Normie had gone over the edge, slithering over the side.

'Come back. Don't be mad.'

It had been different when they were little and stupid and empty-headed, sliding on the seats of their pants, screaming for fear and for joy, not able to understand the danger.

'Normie!'

A wild impulse of loyalty sent Shane scrambling over the side and he was committed before he knew what he had done. Suddenly he was on the slope, fighting for his life, screaming with fear as he used to scream when he was about nine years old, and Normie seen for an instant was clawing somewhere below in a spray of yellow and green. Shane's feet shot from under him and he thudded on his back, arms and legs wide, and the bottom fell out of the earth. He slid screaming in showers of dust and chips of stone and could see nothing but spinning sky from a point outside his body. He seemed to have left his eyes behind. He seemed to be stretching like rubber, yards long, and crashed into scrub, feet first, and crumbled into the ground, burning up as though on fire from head to foot.

He moaned and lay there, foliage and twigs crushed beneath him, too shocked at his own stupidity to move, astonished that he was alive at the bottom of the slag, instead of hanging somewhere by a broken leg, half-way up.

'Normie,' he called thinly, 'are you O.K.?'

Normie was dead or unconscious or gone.

'Normie?'

Shane struggled out of the scrub, burning from abrasions and scratches, feeling suddenly frantic, but Normie was thudding off through the old workings with his draught-horse stride, heading for the road. Shane tried to follow, really tried, but it simply wasn't there. Normie was strong; Normie was terrific; but Shane's legs gave under him and sat him on the ground, on a split and crazed concrete slab as hot as the plate of a stove. The heat was awful there, trapped by the surrounding ruins of Chinaman's Reef Number 5.

Shane sat askew leaning on a hand, head lolling, back sagging in the middle, panting and raw, with a sense of foreboding gathering over him. He knew dust was up there now, driven by higher winds to discolour the sky. The rumble was there, bearing down, bearing against him, heard in spasms between his moans. But why should he be so afraid? Pan Pacific was not the first convoy of vehicles to pass through. The army had gone through once, the real army, in tanks and armoured cars and no one had cared. Recovery teams from the missile testing range hundreds of miles away had gone through another time with a terrific hullabaloo looking for a rocket that had strayed; no one at Chinaman's had turned a hair. Pan Pacific was not a foreign power, the men were not soldiers spraying bullets left and right as they went by. They could only be ordinary fellows doing a job for their pay just like his own Dad. Thinking of these things didn't help; only made it harder to understand.

Maybe if Auntie Sadie hadn't broken the habit of years when she had come to the door of the hall none of it would have happened. If only she had called, 'Everyone here who's going to be here? Good. Come along,' then it would have ended up being a Sunday like the others he knew. She was the one who always said good habit was a rock in a difficult world; break it and beware.

'Normie! Wait for me.'

Normie shouldn't have left him there. He could have fractured a leg or busted his head and Normie wouldn't have cared. He was all steamed up for his Superman act and the rest of the world could go to blazes. That was Normie all over; he was such a child; muscles like a man and a bird brain.

Normie was gone. Leaping through the tussocks towards the road, second wind and all, with a scalding pain like spurs on his backside where sharp stones had ripped the skin but not his jeans. A hand suddenly slapped there, 'Me pants!' But the pants were not torn and flesh mended out of sight without Mum having to perform.

'I'll show 'em. I'll show that Shane. I'll show 'em all. I'll stop them, you'll see. Blooming lip, messing up my Dad's road on a Sunday when he can't damp it down.'

Dust spewing up at a few hundred yards. Any moment now they'd hit the bitumen strip a quarter of a mile from town.

'Making Auntie Sadie cry. Making her criticize my hair, Cherry there and all. Making Auntie Sadie rave. Who do they think they are? Everybody going mad. It's a real nice place without Pan Pacific hanging round. Young blokes coming in, giving Cherry the eye 'cos she's the only decent lookin' girl around. It's bad enough at school with every second fella reckoning he's God's gift to girls, especially to her.'

Faster, Normie. You've got to stop the first one or you'll be stopping none at all. A stitch like cords being drawn together in his side.

'Strike me, I'll die.'

It's a utility truck with flashing red lights and a thumping great sign saying WIDE LOADS FOLLOWING.

'Hey, hey, Pan Pacific, you can't come here.'

Run, Normie. Fly, Normie.

'*Hey!*'

But the truck had gone on its way. Streaming up the bitumen strip into town, dust flaking from it like snow; and Normie fell at the roadside on knees and elbows, exhausted and dazed.

A horn started blowing from a distance, blaring down towards him, blaring at him. 'Get out of the way,' it demanded, 'shift your bones.'

'Blurts,' groaned Normie, 'what more do you want? You've got the road.'

The horn blaring at him, bearing down, not believing that a puny mortal would presume to question its right of way; brakes suddenly hissing and squealing with urgency and surprise.

Leah could feel something coming, something she couldn't grasp or understand; like hysteria or panic or pain intent upon thrusting itself at her. Her head was numbed with prophecies of doom, with the dreadful words of part of the Psalm she had learned, about death feeding on people, about houses and dwelling places perishing. There was a feeling growing in her of being singled out, of being pushed aside, of being left on her own to stand against a force of overwhelming power.

The others were there, of course they were; the women, the young children, the men, but she was alone in the midst of them, the odd one out. Her mother and father had gone to the phone and Shane she couldn't see. No one really mattered but Shane.

'It'll be turned into a great big grave.'

There wouldn't be a town. She wouldn't have a home. They'd go away, the Elliots in one direction and Shane in another.

It was awful being alone in a crowd. The others all leant on each other in a hidden sort of way and drew closer and closer together not meaning to exclude her but somehow squeezing her aside. Or perhaps she had been standing apart all the time and had only thought she had belonged to that sullen crowd at the edge of town waiting for the dust to divulge its mysteries. Something inhuman, far more terrible than Pan Pacific, was clanking nearer and nearer like a gigantic ball and chain. Nothing was distinct. Nothing had sharp edges. Everything was blurred, even the imagined ball on the plain. She seemed to see Chinaman's Reef as if it lay at a great distance across wastes of time, saw everyone in it except Shane, all the dead people of other years as well as those alive, and saw herself holding back the gigantic ball, underneath it, desolate and alone, almost like Atlas bowed beneath the weight of the world. But the ball was too huge, too heavy; it teetered on top of her, bearing down with tremendous weight, threatening to crush her, and no one else cared, not even Shane because he wasn't there.

Huge words and blinking lights suddenly confronted her. DANGER. WIDE LOADS FOLLOWING. Appearing out of nowhere, out of the mists of her imaginings. They were real. They were solid. They were there. And she felt an uncontrollable and terrifying compulsion to live her dream through to the end. Her body hit the road but no one rushed to her aid. No one screamed, 'Leah!' No one dragged her away. They left her to bear it alone. Nothing happened at all and the dream turned suddenly to a horror of injury and death. She shielded herself with kicking legs and arms and frantically jerked herself clear, and when she looked up, wildly, nothing was there. She was completely alone.

She whimpered, bewildered and hurt because no one had seen and no one had cared.

The blinking lights and the huge words were reversing swiftly away, the driver of the vehicle looking backwards, head and shoulder out through the window looking back up the road, and not a living person was looking her way in a hundred yards. All were heading out of town, and there was a lot of noise, engines, horns blowing, people shouting.

Her sob rose up and she ran home.

Normie, on hands and elbows, drooped on his piece of roadside, groaning for breath, muttering passionate threats against the squealing brakes and horn blasts.

'Blurts,' he hissed, 'with knobs on.'

'You,' demanded an angry voice, 'can't you read? Get off the road. Do you want to be killed, you silly little fool?'

Normie twisted his head and viewed a wheel of enormous size. He blinked at it, dismayed, astonished to find it there, almost nudging his side. The rest of the vehicle, a distorted perspective, was a nightmare of angles and masses bigger than anything he had ever seen on wheels. It snorted and belched out fumes. It shuddered, it sighed. It was thick with dust from stem to stern. Pieces of scrub torn from narrow roadsides were lodged in its crevices. Up high two smeared black circles looked down; a face, a dust-encrusted head without hair; two black spectacle lenses instead of eyes.

'Come on, come on. Out of the way.'

Another horn was blaring, bearing down, and Normie seethed with sudden rage.

'Whose road do you think it is?' he screamed. 'It's my Dad's!'

'I'll tan your hide, kid, if you don't get out of the way.'

'You and who else?' screamed Normie.

A door squealed open, grating over gravel on the step thrown up from numerous miles of road, and two legs dropped to the ground on the far side. They walked round to the front. They belonged to a dirty-looking man at least six feet high, but not to the man with black lenses instead of eyes.

'What are you lying there for?'

'Don't argue with him,' said the voice from up top, 'get him off the road.'

'Come on, lad. Make it snappy. We're not out for a Sunday drive.' He was not an unpleasant man, but he was hot and haggard and seemed nervous of the driver in sun-glasses. Horns were blaring and dust on the breeze was rolling in like a fog.

'What is it, lad? Are you sick?'

'No,' scowled Normie.

'Well come on then, get up. You'll cause a pile-up back there.'

Normie wasn't scared of him; no sir; he could see that he was not the type of man who would be quick with his hands. 'If I want to stop here I can. It's a free country. I'm not breakin' any laws. I'm not on the road.'

'Look, lad, it's not fun driving these things. We're tired.' He hooked his thumb. 'And so's everyone back there. We want to get where we're going.'

'I'm not stoppin' you. Get, why don't you!'

'Don't argue with him,' shouted the voice from up top, 'God help him if I have to come down.'

'Come on, lad. Don't push us too far.'

'Push you?' Normie shrieked. 'I'm minding my own business, standing on the side of the road.' He got up, seething, but didn't give an inch of the line he had occupied. 'Who's pushing who? Not me.' Shane was getting close, wading through the tussocks like someone crossing a stream. Normie could feel him there, all consternation, all eyes and ears. 'I'm not on the road; I'm on the side.'

'We're not saying you're not on the side, but we've got a wide load! You'll get hit! Stand back to the edge or I'll have to put you there!'

'You won't touch me,' shrieked Normie. 'I live here. This is my bit of road. What happens if a car comes along? What happens then? Do I take up as much room as a car? *You* move over, I'm stoppin' right here!'

'Don't argue with him,' shouted the voice from up top, 'he's only a kid. Are you scared of a kid? Give him the push.'

Horns still blared, dust still rolled down, the door of another vehicle suddenly slammed, and the tall man moved a step towards Normie.

'Don't you touch me,' shrieked Normie, 'I've got witnesses. Shane! Shane!'

Shane came through on to the road, almost numb with fear,

feeling about two feet high, and Normie's hand was reaching for him, groping wildly for him, without looking. 'Shane!'

'I'm here!'

'Don't you touch me,' shrieked Normie. 'Shane's here. We know the law. My Dad tells me.'

The tall man cut off his stride, dropped his hands and swore, and the driver with sun-glasses shouted, 'Get back inside. Let's go. Let them argue with thirty tons of steel.' The engine revved, coughing out fumes, and two more men came pacing up from the rear. Shane darted to Normie, grabbing at his hand, trying to pull him away. 'They'll run over you.'

'They won't,' Normie shrieked, 'they wouldn't dare.'

Another voice called, 'What are these boys doing here?'

The huge prime mover lurched on its gears. 'Normie, Normie, come away,' but Normie broke Shane's grip with an angry swing and pushed him off. 'I won't move. I'm not going to move. If they want to pass me they can back up and go round.'

The engine sighed again, dying down, and the man with sun-glasses hung an arm through the cab window and beat his fist against the door; the two men from the rear brushed past Shane and each lifted Normie by an armpit bodily from the ground and dumped him kicking and yelling off the road. Gears instantly thudded again and the vehicle moved, but a voice like a bull bellowed down the road, 'Take your hands off those kids; if it's a fight you want try us for size.'

Dead centre, booming up the road from town, like warriors emerging out of dust, came Normie's father and Shane's father, and Cherry's father lagging twenty yards or so behind. Normie knew they were there, couldn't see them, but heard his father's roar. He spun out of the tussocks like a terrier, dodging the two men, and threw himself back to the position he had held before, now hard against the edge of the low-loader where its second forward lurch had been arrested by the driver.

'Dad,' Shane yelled, 'they're trying to run Normie over.'

'They wouldn't dare,' screeched Normie, with his teeth bared. 'I'm stickin' to this bit o' road. It's our road, not theirs. They put their hands on me, Dad. They assaulted me like it is in the law. You tell 'em, Dad.'

Albert Muir's huge hand seemed to reach out from yards away to alight on the shoulder of his son. He moved so fast he seemed suddenly to have been there all the time. 'O.K., O.K., leave these kids alone.' He was a big man, he knew his own strength, and didn't easily scare. When muscle power was called for he knew exactly how far to go.

Stan Baxter was suddenly beside Shane.

Cherry's father, with an uncomfortable sense of danger, stood in the centre of the road, arms folded, inches from the massive bumper bar of the prime mover, and nervously set his jaw.

The driver in sun-glasses shouted down, 'What is this? You're obstructing the road. Is everyone round here mad?'

Engines were stopping. Doors were slamming. Dust was drifting away. Shane was aware of an irregular line of blinking lights and a build-up of prime movers and trailers and caravans like a railway train. Groups of men were coming up the roadside from the rear. The utility truck that had gone ahead to town was reversing back again under considerable power, trailed by women and children.

The driver in sun-glasses shouted down, 'Clear the road!'

'I stopped you,' hissed Normie with joy, 'you're not busting in here.'

'Nobody clears anything,' barked Albert Muir. 'I don't care if you're the men from Mars.'

'You'll care all right,' someone yelled, 'when the police get here.'

'What police? There's not a policeman in forty miles.'

'We've got rights. We've got priority. We've been getting here for three days.'

'Bully for you,' boomed Normie's Dad, 'but you've got no priority here. You occupy your fair share of road and we occupy ours.

There was a pressure of men, a sense of heat and anger and crowd. The utility truck, rushing up in reverse, stopped a few yards away. Shane shivered and sought his father's eyes. Even Normie was aware of the odds suddenly getting out of hand; his dad had fought some mighty fights but they were a long time ago; his dad had been in gaol for a day for breaking a barman's ribs with a single punch but that had been in 1953. And Shane's dad and Cherry's dad couldn't have fought a hole in a paper bag.

A new voice of a different tone called from behind. 'What's the hold-up? *Into* the town, I said.'

'These characters say they won't move, Mr Gibbs.'

'Do they?' A man of authority pressed through. He was unhurried and cool. His shirt was almost clean, his hair was grey, and he had travelled in an air-conditioned car. 'Who won't move?'

'We won't move,' declared Albert Muir, 'and we've got you on assault already. Two of your lackeys manhandled my boy. You'll not intimidate us, Mister.'

The man called Gibbs looked around, ignoring the threat, taking his time. 'Who are these people?'

The driver of the utility truck descriptively waved an arm. 'They live here. There's a horde of women and kids back there.'

'You're dead right there is,' boomed Albert Muir.

Gibbs remained unhurried, with disconcerting calm. 'Well, they'll have to strike camp, won't they, and move on.'

'Strike *camp*?' bellowed Albert Muir. 'I've lived here since the day I was born. We've got rights, too.'

Gibbs sighed. 'These bush lawyers make me tired. They're always half-baked. I say he's trespassing on private property, which is a blunter way of stating it than I had hoped. But, if he wants to play it tough! Drive on, Kennedy. Drive through. They'll move.'

Gibbs turned suddenly on the Muirs, father and son, meeting them for the first time in the eye. 'If we're to split hairs in this nasty little way, don't throw the Mining Act at me. In this place it comes unstuck. This was always a Company town and always a Company road. Every square yard of ground and every foot of road for farther than your eyes can see. You leased your houses and were permitted to use the road. It's all in the title deeds, *Mister*, our titles, and it's never been changed. You're trespassing. Out of our way.'

'Dad,' cried Normie, 'what's he say?'

'What he says, Normie.' Albert Muir was not the big man any more. He knew. He had always known. So had every other adult in town. 'It can't be the spirit of the law but it's suited too many people for too many years. It's why it's been a strip of dust and not a proper road.' All the fire had gone from Albert Muir. 'Someone's been paying the Shire for forty years to have it maintained. Pan Pacific, I suppose.' He seemed to sag as though the effort of standing erect was more than he could manage. 'We can't fight it, son. Like the man says, on this bit of road we've got to let him through.'

'Dad?' breathed Shane. 'Don't we live here now?' The response was a heavy arm that came to rest across his shoulders.

Cherry's father stepped clear of the prime mover, turned from it, and started walking back to town, towards the women and children whose dark and brooding stillness was unlike an Australian scene.

CHAPTER SEVEN

Pan Pacific, Go Away

CHERRY waited in the shade of Auntie Sadie's verandah, sitting gingerly on the edge of an ottoman couch tattered by weather and wear and faded by decades of sunshine to the colour of old paper. It was Jack's couch, not often used by humans. Dog hairs, black and grey, encircled a greasy hollow a few inches from her. It looked like a bird's nest. It was Jack's nest for long summer days and cool evenings. It was alive with fleas, but Cherry's blood was not to their taste. She waited on Auntie Sadie with a tremble greater than ordinary nervousness.

'Hurry up,' she whispered. 'Why are you so long? You know I'm here. What are you doing?'

But the house was quiet (Auntie Sadie, imagined in a grove of shadows and ornate table legs, witch-like invoking supernatural powers). The only living sound drifting close was Jack's wheezing breath, Jack on guard like a heraldic lion behind the screen door. Cherry waited and waited, for hours, for days; it seemed as though she had been there for ever while a rumbling world of bewildering tensions underwent bewildering changes.

Dust blew from the sky, blew away. Paleness and cleanness came back, immensity and silence, creaking heat and stillness, cicadas and magpie calls; but no engines, no rumble, no dust. Extraordinary aching stillness with Jack breathing like a grampus. (What was a grampus?) Jack breathing like an old clock grating between the seconds dragging across the years. Main Street stretched out throbbing with emptiness.

'Auntie Sadie; hurry up, will you!'

A great big hole, imagined, out of which a world was being bitten by machines with wide-open jaws crashing down on jointed necks of steel and sinews of cable, teeth of iron cruelly

67

curved like those of the sabre-toothed beast in the encyclopaedia. Beside the hole a mountain of rubble growing day by
day with tree trunks sticking out of it and rafters and broken
bricks and television masts and bedsteads and lumps of road
once patched by her Dad and the gate she had swung on since
she was old enough to climb. The gate the boys came to in the
evening to listen to the piano. Ronnie Garrett might have come
one day too. Sometimes Ronnie looked at her and she knew.
Sometimes she was realistic and knew differently. She was
Normie's girl because Normie said so. She was Shane's girl too
(not hard to guess), though he never said it aloud. She was
Dad's girl as well. Everybody's girl but Ronnie Garrett's,
except when he glanced at her, slightly frowning, for a second
or two in the bus going to school, or in the bus coming home, or
when his shoulder brushed against hers (accidentally?) on
Sunday mornings. Ronnie was a cut above the crowd; his
world was three miles and a gap away. She played the piano in
the evening but he never came to hear. The piano was sticking
out of the rubble mountain too. Dad had bought it for her
when she was nine, after he had sold the lease for eleven
hundred dollars to Ronnie's father. Through contacts arranged
by Mr Elliot they had bought a superseded television set and a
mast, a second-hand generator, a three-volume encyclopaedia
and an old piano. ('The kid's got talent; we owe it to her.')
Now the piano, making horrible sounds, was buried in the
rubble and Chinaman's Reef was a great big hole.

Leah cried on her bed, into the face of her pillow, and her
father's hand rattled the knob of her door.

'Leah! We're not judging you because you broke the phone;
but you've got to unlock your door.' His voice was muffled as
though belonging to another place or another time. There were
too many confusions inside her to allow for the precise meaning
of words.

'You haven't got to hide from us, Leah. We're not going to
hurt you. We'll certainly have questions to answer, because it *is*
the Post Office phone, but we've got the phone box, lass. We
can ring out and we can get messages in. We've got to get in

touch with the Shire, at least, to clarify our position here. Leah! Please!' He rattled the knob. 'Madge, she's not going to open up. It's terribly awkward. What on earth are we to do?'

'Look, dear,' Mrs Elliot said, 'we've got to pull together. This is not like you. It's a crisis for us all and we're not going to get anywhere until you apologize to Miss Clapp. She shouts us down; we can't get a word in edgeways; she cuts us off. I know she's impossible, but she's our one link with the outside world. She'll take no calls from us until you apologize. You'll have to do it, Leah. She's on duty all day and we can't get past her. She says she's taken all the lip she's going to stand from kids at Chinaman's on the phone.'

Knuckles knocked on the door.

'Leah; do you hear me? Leah; open up. Don't behave like a child.'

The door rattled. Someone sighed.

'Go round to the window.'

'That'll do no good. The blind's drawn, the window's closed. *Leah!* I'm getting cross.'

'Miss Clapp says she will not provide a service, and is not compelled to, when offensive language is directed against the operator. She says you swore. She says you've got to say you're sorry. Leah, did you swear?'

'You know I didn't swear. I never swear. It's not true.'

'She says she heard every word.'

'I don't care what she heard. I didn't swear. She's a liar. Anyway, she couldn't have heard on a broken phone. And I couldn't care less about Miss Clapp and I couldn't care less about the phone. I want to be left alone.'

'You can't always have what you want, my dear.'

'Do I ever have what I want?'

'For pity's sake, Leah. What's got into you?'

Her father explained, 'Miss Clapp can hear us, child, on the Post Office phone, but we can't hear her. That's why we're using the outside phone, to hear *her*. We didn't know you were in the house. We never dreamt you'd come sneaking in along the lane. All this could have been settled minutes ago. We're letting everyone down. People relying on us for information and two stupid females sitting on their dignity, *you and her!*'

'Leah,' Mrs Elliot said, 'your father will break down the door if you don't open up at once.'

'I don't know about that, Madge.'

'She's disgracing us and I'll not be disgraced. Break it down, Bill. Put your shoulder to it. It's rotten enough to give at a touch.'

'She's crying, Madge. She's a good girl.'

'Are you going to do it or am I?'

The door burst open, decently on its hinges, and they came in, but saw her in the breathless gloom lying face down, only her head turned, as if gasping for air. They stopped short of her and suddenly her mother dropped to her knees beside the bed, her hand falling gently to the small of Leah's back. 'What's wrong, darling?' The woman's anger was gone; her mood was changed.

'Oh, Mummy, it doesn't matter. It's just me.'

'In what way, darling? Are you sick? You mustn't get yourself into a state like this.'

'I never do anything right. I'm such a fool. I'm only good for reading aloud from something that's written down.'

The woman grimaced. 'Bill, what does she mean? What's she talking about? Leah, you've got to explain.'

'I don't want them to dig up the town.'

'We don't want them to either, darling.'

'My room.'

'Yes, dear.'

'Shane.'

'What about Shane?'

'That horrible Miss Clapp doesn't even care what it means.'

'That's not the point, dear. Whether she cares or whether she doesn't, she's making things awkward for us all.'

'I threw myself down on the road to stop them, Mum. I offered my life and they didn't even look. They just backed away. They didn't even know I was there.'

'I think she's hysterical. That's the trouble in this place, Bill Elliot. You can never get the doctor until you're dead.'

'I'm not sick, Mum.' Leah rolled over, dislodging her mother's hand, and sat up, not really feeling anything, listening to herself as if her voice were another person's. 'I'll tell her, Mum. I'll tell Miss Clapp.'

'Not *tell* her, darling. Apologize.'

'Yes, Mum. That's right.'

'Bill, I think she ought to stay in bed. Are you all right, dear? You're acting so strangely.'

'She's got to go to the phone.'

'There's no *got to* about it. If I say she stays in bed she stays. I think you'd better ring the doctor.'

'How?'

'What do you mean—how?'

'Her Majesty Miss Clapp will not accept a call.'

'I don't need a doctor, Mum.' Leah tugged a handkerchief from her sleeve and loudly blew her nose. 'I'm all right. No, you don't have to hold me up. Please, Mum, let me go. I'll tell her I'm sorry. I'll lick her shoes.'

'You don't have to put it that way, dear. That sounds terrible.'

'Well, it *is* terrible,' Bill Elliot muttered, but Leah had gone and they had to hurry after her. 'For me I don't care what she said; I don't care if she did swear; the kid had every right in the world. That woman's riding for a fall.'

'I doubt it. Her kind get away with it. The devil looks after his own.'

Leah heard their voices and the things they said and found herself in the phone box—a miracle of locomotion; not knowing how she got there—with her parents pressing close holding back the door, letting in a little air. Inside the phone box it must have been a hundred and forty degrees. The handpiece was hot, as if a coal glowed in its core, and she was miserably aware of a chewed fingernail pressed to the dial. Her father was saying, 'Dial the number, Leah. Dial 04. They're coming back. See, they're coming back along the road and we haven't a thing to tell them. I haven't even spoken to the Shire Engineer and there's no more news on the wireless until half-past twelve. I don't often wish people ill, but something's got to be done about that woman.'

Leah felt sick, not because of the heat, but because of 'that woman' and of Auntie Sadie, too. 'They're not answering,' she said. 'It's not ringing.'

'Hang up and dial again.'

'It sounds dead to me, Dad.'

'It couldn't be. She wouldn't. Here, give it to me.'

'Oh, Dad, I'm so sorry, and I don't suppose I've ever been really rude to anyone before.'

He sighed and took the phone and dialled 04, his pale anger giving him a yellowed hue. 'It couldn't be dead,' he hissed. 'She wouldn't dare.' He cracked the handset back on the hook. 'By the living Harry, I'm not taking this lying down. What did I say to her, Madge? I told her we'd stand for so much and no more. I'll take the van. I'll go to Kenyon. Open cut mining. Miss flaming Clapp. Who the devil does she think she is? We may all be nobodies in Chinaman's Reef, but they're going to know we're here.'

Shane looked back with misery and with hatred. He looked back and stared through the following crowd. Somehow or other he had got out in front on his own.

Pan Pacific hadn't moved. Pan Pacific had become a mass of machinery lying silent beyond a distant group of hostile strangers on the road. They were hundreds of yards away but they had grouped like men at an open-air meeting, a few of them moving about as though spreading ideas. Something about it puzzled Shane. Something about it was strange.

His mother came towards him (as though walking out of a memory of other days), clasping at the front of her dressing-gown with a white hand. She was still carrying her towel. Her hair was a frizz of sun-dried foam.

'Come on, Shane,' she said, 'looking daggers at them won't frighten them away.'

'It's not fair, Mum.'

'No, dear, it's not. Come along.'

'I could spit in their eye.'

'That's what Normie did, isn't it? That's what Mr Muir did, isn't it? Where's it got us? As if I cared. They're bigger than we are. We know that now. Normie and his Dad made sure.'

'You're not going to give up, Mum, like that?'

He saw her eyes turn oddly; he saw the whites of her eyes; her lips became a line. It was a sad look, a peculiar kind of

sneer that had nothing to do with the nice things of motherhood
he knew, that belonged to some other department of her life he
had never seen. The look said: 'You're a child. You bother me.
You don't understand.' Then she walked on and away. They all
walked on and away. He had been in front for a while on his
own; now he was behind. Or take another view. All were
retreating, even Normie, but Shane had dug in his heels. Suddenly he despised the spirit that could send them slinking home.

'They're not going to do it,' he said aloud. 'God won't let
them. I know. You tell me how to stop them, God, and I'll do
it. You'll see. The very idea. Digging up the town, they say. An
open cut, they say. Carting it off to the coast. Shipping it to
Japan. They might as well be an army; they might as well blow
us up with bombs; it's just the same.'

He stood alone in the centre of the road. He could see the hall
where the day began. He could see the Slag and the tall chimney stack of Chinaman's Reef Number 5 where he had played
the games of boyhood. The stinging pain of his crazy slide from
the top of the Slag to the ground had gone. Quite gone. That
was symbolic; he wasn't frightened any more. He could see
Pan Pacific drawn up in battle-line.

'I'm going back,' he thought. 'I'll stick a spanner in their
works, somehow.'

Main Street wasn't empty now. People came drifting into
Cherry's view, some in the shade of overhanging trees and only
partly seen, glimpses of legs and bodies decapitated by black
shadow, some in the sun-splash down the middle, all drifting like
leaves on a quiet stream going nowhere and not caring.

'Oh, people,' a voice inside her cried, 'is it really that bad?'

Almost everyone who lived in town drifted into view, some
looking back as though they expected traffic to run them down,
some limply holding hands, one man on his own, Mr Muir,
slouching, head bowed. It was like a mime and she had to guess
the names and the words. The only words that seemed to fit
were ones that went with tears.

'Can't you stop them, Dad? Isn't there anything you can do?
You can't let them dig it up. It'll be such a shame.'

She wanted to run to them, to be strong, to be a mother to them all, even to her Dad who hurt so easily, whose mouth turned down when he was sad. Dad wasn't very bright, though Mum said he had been as sharp as a tack years ago. There'd be nothing he could do. She tried very hard to go to them, but she was scared and her body wouldn't move.

'Auntie Sadie. You're the strong one. You couldn't still be praying. Golly, if He hasn't heard by now He'll never hear.'

Pan Pacific lying like a gigantic storm about to happen on the far side of town, not seen from Auntie Sadie's verandah, lying there dark and ominous. Lying there shapeless. She couldn't even imagine its form. Perhaps a huge centipede of iron, miles long, with the brain of a malevolent man. Breathing. Wheezing like the dog Jack as it breathed.

The people like leaves now caught in an eddy outside the store. A large, sloppy woman with hands on hips (Normie's Mum) looking back, a wiry, bony man scuffing his boot hopelessly as he walked along the road (Shane's Dad), boys and girls moving into the shade, dissolving from sight. The eddy gone; no one there at all; Cherry sadly feeling a sense of loss. Mrs Elliot must have made tea. 'Come in out of the sun,' she'd say, 'and we'll all have a cup of tea. There's cordial for the children. Where's Cherry?'

'Gone to Auntie Sadie's, Mum,' Leah would say. 'She's been gone an awfully long time. Do you think I'd better go and see?'

But Leah would only be trying to get out of the way; she was nervous in a crowd.

Jack's breath like a grating clock grinding the minutes away.

'Gee whiz, Auntie Sadie, get up off your knees. I can't wait all day. Do you think He's going to strike them dead with a bolt of lightning from the sky? There's not a cloud up there.'

Silence from Pan Pacific; an awful, aching, threatening silence. Why weren't they battering into town knocking things down?

Silence from Auntie Sadie.

Main Street as quiet as the grave.

Not a sign of Leah.

'Come on, Leah. Surely someone's going to come. What

about you, Normie? I thought I was your girl. Have you forgotten I'm alive? Here's your chance, Shane.'

A clock started chiming from deep in the house, as though chiming in a tomb. Sounding rather sinister. As though Auntie Sadie had died on her knees and only the clock knew. An awful thought and a passing panic.

She counted twelve. The morning had gone.

On any other Sunday she would have been home again, changed out of her frock into a washed-out red blouse tucked racily into her jeans, setting the table for the midday meal. Dad would be sharpening the knife on the steel, Mum would be sucking through her teeth from the heat of the oven door, Peter would be begging for the crackly bits of fat that Dad would never serve (except to himself) from the roast of lamb. 'No, Peter; fat's not good for you.' (There wasn't a wisp of smoke from a chimney in town; except perhaps from the store; all the ovens would be going cold, all the dinners would be off the boil.) At about one-thirty Normie would call. Shane would come hot on his heels. Usually Leah too in her special, shy way. Perhaps they'd walk to the Devil's Kitchen, a hole in the plain, out towards Garrett's a couple of miles, with a few of the small fry tagging along behind, darting from bush to bush, making Normie mad. He hated the little kids hanging round; he hated it worse when they crept on him unawares. If ever he held Cherry by the hand his sisters, the horrible 'twins', always told. Once a single titter had given the crowd away when Normie had been kissing Cherry while Shane and Leah had been trying to look unconcerned. (Leah, really, was a scream.) Normie had chased the little kids for about a mile threatening he'd kill them if they told. They told. Oddly, the grown-ups smiled, which sort of suggested, Normie said, that the kiss had been invented in olden days when Dad was a boy. Sometimes they caught perch in the Devil's Kitchen and took them home for tea; bamboo for rods, corks for floats, and wriggling earthworms. Permanent water was there and huge boulders and goats gone wild and about a million birds, sometimes even kangaroos suddenly surprised. There were tiger snakes but not the biting kind; perhaps they knew the kids by sight and had never heard about the trouble with Eve. Cherry's eyes filled with tears.

There'd be no more Sunday afternoons of that kind; they were gone too. A wide, wide plain and a handful of kids running free. They'd be stuck in a big town. They'd be stuck in a cage.

Oh, Pan Pacific, go away.

'Miss Stevenson,' she wailed, 'I'm waiting for you. Don't you remember I'm here?'

They had dawdled into Elliot's Store like mourners after a burial, certain of a great loss, but uncertain of its breadth, glimpsing of its meaning only the fact that something enormous had gone. As though yesterday had been wiped from human memory and tomorrow would never come.

'Bill's out the back changing his clothes,' Mrs Elliot had said. 'I think he'd like a hearing.'

So they dawdled in and sprawled on stools, on the floor, on the counter, on bags of grain, displacing the cats, sitting or leaning, self-consciously acting out their parts, women frowning silent the hopes of younger children for ice-creams. 'It's Sunday,' Mrs Muir hissed, 'the shop's shut.'

'The door's open, Mummy. We're in here, aren't we? Mrs Elliott won't mind.'

'What the dickens is old Bill changing his clothes for?'

She was thinking of filling ice-cream cones; Bill probably would have done the same. 'Going through to Kenyon, he says, to stir things up. Someone's got to do it, Owen.'

Cherry's father sighed.

But their sadness was also an act that they played on the surface, believing it to be the right and proper front to show. 'Thanks for the ice-cream, Mrs Elliot.' 'You shouldn't have done it, Madge; there was no need.' They were too dazed to feel deeply anything at all; even the furrowed lines of thought on grown-up brows masked empty minds. Where could you start? What was there to do? If the edge of the cliff gave way you simply had to fall until you hit the ground. Maybe, then, you might scrape yourself together and stagger on your way. Maybe it would be better if you died.

'We stopped them,' Normie said, 'didn't we, Dad?' But Normie didn't get an answer and blushed at the wall, briefly concentrating on the telephone broken there. Normie had a feeling that the men had let him down. Surely if one kid could stop them, three men could send them away. But Pan Pacific had stood firm. He was sore too. His backside was raw, probably bleeding a treat from his slide down the Slag. There'd be the devil to pay if blood started showing through. He leant his back against the counter trying to trace the coursing blood with the ends of his nerves and fighting the urge to thrust down his hand to explore. What an awful way to die, bleeding to death (in secret) from a cut on your backside. He knew what Leah would say if she knew. 'It's a judgment on you, see, for being crude to girls.' Leah was looking ghastly over there near the back door, as though she should have been in the bathroom being sick into the pan. What was Leah thinking? Would any boy ever know? She was a born old maid, another of Auntie Sadie's kind.

'I'm hostile,' Cherry's mother said but sounded like a little girl. 'Have you got a cigarette, Stan?'

'You don't smoke, Rose.'

'I know,' she said, sounding frail, 'but it's the way I feel. Last time I had a cigarette was in the war when the *Centaur* went down. My sister was a nurse on that ship, you know. She drowned. One cigarette I smoked. Silly way to say goodbye.'

'What happened to your phone calls, Madge?'

Mrs Elliot managed to answer without looking anyone in the eye, without raising her voice or hurting Leah. 'When Leah dropped the phone I'm afraid she did some damage to the line.'

'You didn't get through?'

'No.'

'There's the public phone.'

'You saw us there. We tried it and it's the same.'

'It's so blamed sudden,' exploded Albert Muir. 'We've just got to have rights. In they come and out we go. It's mad. Auntie Sadie's let us down and Garrett's got something to answer for. He must have been tying up the deal for years. It's more than copper they're going for. There must be something else down there.'

'Copper's riding pretty high.'

'Not that high, Stan.'

'Look Albert, when the mine flooded copper wasn't worth a

cent. It did them a favour, didn't it? Leaving the town to rot
was cheaper than starting up again. If they had no heart then,
are they likely to have one now? It's still the same company;
don't be fooled by names. You know what the old-timers
reckoned about that flooding. Grandpa Baxter for one. That
flooding stinks, he used to say.' Shane's father went silent then,
and tight-lipped. It was a particularly difficult matter to talk
about.

'What are they doing out there, anyway?' Albert Muir
stamped to the door. 'Why don't they get on with it?'

'I said we stopped them, Dad, didn't I?' shrilled Normie.

Shane's mother flared. 'If I hear that from you again, young
man, you'll feel the back of my hand.'

Albert Muir looked sharply round, taken by surprise, as they
all were. 'Hey,' he said, with an odd inflection that faded away.
She was a sweet woman, Mrs Baxter, that kind of manner
wasn't her style. His sense of shock turned against Normie.
'Yes,' he said, 'say it again and you'll feel my hand, too. You
didn't solve any problems out there, lad, throwing yourself
round on the road. You made 'em! *I've never felt so helpless in all
my life!*' He barged on to the road, the screen door slamming,
again banging his fist into his thigh.

Mrs Elliot put an ice-cream cone into Normie's hand. 'Here
you are, love,' she said, 'don't feel too bad. Whatever you did,
at least you tried. It wasn't the right way, that's all.'

Normie could have collapsed in tears but had no idea his
misery showed so plainly. Leah felt for him a sudden, com-
passionate urge. Normie had tried; so had she. Leah had never
felt anything much for Normie before, except indifference or
distrust or fear. Normie was rude, like a third-rate comedian,
not like Shane. And thinking of Shane she looked suddenly for
him, but couldn't see him anywhere. Her father came in with
quick steps from the rear, in his best suit and hat, his face
shining and snicked from a hurried shave, sweat already
beading his neck and brow. 'Dear,' his wife exclaimed, 'not
your suit! Use your brains. You'll fry.'

Perhaps he wondered why Mrs Baxter had her head turned
away, perhaps he realized Mrs Muir was biting back words in
defence of her son that could only start another row, perhaps he

heard Mrs Cooper coughing over her cigarette, perhaps he counted all the ice-creams served free of charge. Perhaps he had no thought other than his own. 'I hope we're not taking this like lambs. I've got my mad up. If Pan Pacific's not enough, this flaming Miss Clapp's the last straw. They're treating us like a lot of bush-whackers. We're not going to be pushed around and we can't wait for Sadie Stevenson to show her hand—*if* she means to move at all. I don't know about you people, but I'm having the Shire President out here, I'm having the Shire Secretary out here, I'm having a big lump of that Engineer. And Miss flaming Clapp I'm personally emptying into the Memorial Horse Trough, curling pins and all. Who's with me, or do I go it alone?'

Albert Muir bulked in shadow against the screen door from the outside. 'What's Miss Clapp got to do with it?'

Leah's mother sighed. 'Oh, Bill, I didn't tell them. What was the use of upsetting Leah?'

The back door clicked and Leah was gone.

Bill Elliot frowned at the empty area of wall where his daughter had been, then glanced sharply at his wife. 'Don't follow her! Let her go!' At times he was an assertive man. 'That woman,' he said passionately, 'is persecuting our little girl. She says Leah swore. If Leah used strong words I'll bet she had cause. She demands an apology. Leah offered to give it. But Kenyon Exchange has closed the line. Does that answer your question? I don't know what she said and I don't care. I'm going to Kenyon. Who's with me?'

'What are you going to achieve?' cried Shane's mother. 'You'll only get angry. You'll make it worse.'

'Worse than *what*?'

Albert Muir came inside. 'We've got to get someone on our side. The Shire seems the best bet. Pan Pacific can't possibly steam into town and start knocking it over. They've got to give us a day or two. They can't chuck us out cold. I'll come with you, Bill, but no fireworks, understand. Let's take it calm, like Dorrie Baxter says. Let's drive nice and easy to Kenyon and simmer down.'

Normie squealed, 'How do you get round that mob up the road?'

Albert Muir raised his brows. 'It's a point. You'll never get past 'em, Bill. They're all over the road.'

'I'll go out the back way and cut across the stock route. I'll get round. I promise that much, but nothing more. I'm telling you, if I want to lose my temper I'll bally well lose it. I've got business here. Nineteen years I've carried this dump on my back, Lord alone knows how. Are you lot likely to square me up? Can you see yourselves paying off what you owe? Can you see me starting up again, somewhere else, at my age, with my asthma, on the strength of your I.O.U's?'

'Break it down, Bill,' Cherry's father grumbled.

'Can any one of you blokes see himself starting up again, anywhere, any time? You're not the right kind. I'm counting myself in, too. We've got our little rackets. It's too cosy here. We get along very nicely in our quiet way. Sure, we've got problems; who hasn't? Sure we're stony broke; but who'd change?'

Shane's father said, 'Give us five minutes for a scrub and a change of clothes and I'll meet you on the road. Can you squeeze us in, Bill? You're with us, aren't you, Owen? Let's make a deputation of it. Two of us are better than one. Four are better than two.'

'A deputation?' Bill Elliot's expression was that of a satisfied man. 'That's what I've been getting at, all along. Five minutes, you blokes. I'll meet you on the road.'

'At dinner time!' Mrs Muir protested. 'You can't go without food. You'll be away all day.'

'Let's see some sandwiches then, cut in double-quick time!'

'You won't find people on a Sunday,' Shane's mother complained. 'They'll be playing golf. They'll be visiting their posh friends. They don't live in our sort of world, not those people. What are we to them?' She had given up; she was feeling very low; or that was how it seemed.

'We'll find them,' growled Bill Elliot, 'we'll find 'em, mark my word.'

'Can I come too?' Normie shrilled.

'One of you should stay,' Mrs Muir said. 'There should be a man. You can't leave women on their own to face a crowd like that.'

'Sit on them, dear. You'll squash them flat.'

'Can I come, too?' Normie shrilled once more.

But no one heard or else considered he had already commanded more attention than he deserved. All crowded for the doors, except his sisters, the horrible 'twins', born apart by a year and a day, who thought the hand was quicker than the eye. They snatched at chewing-gum from the counter stand and scuttled for their lives. But Normie hardly cared. With underwear stuck by blood to his skin he had enough worries of his own. And to be dismissed from adult company without a word after leading them to war left a different kind of wound that hurt even more.

Suddenly the shop was empty and Normie was on his own.

'Miserable so-and-so's,' he sulked. 'Telling me off. Making me feel small. Taking no notice of me. I'm the one that stopped Pan Pacific. I stopped them back there and they're still there. All they did was mess it up. All they did was walk away. All they did was tell me I'd feel the weight of their hands as if I was a little kid.' He wriggled wretchedly in his underwear. 'Blooming bleeding to death. They wouldn't care if they knew.' He waddled like a duck with legs apart to the door. 'I don't believe that phone doesn't work. Doesn't work, my eye. They're trying to pull a fast one. They're scared to fight Pan Pacific on their own. My blooming Dad; what a disappointment he turns out to be. Running off to Kenyon to get someone to hold his hand. I'd stop them. I'd stop the cows. I'd tell 'em to hop it or get pumped full of lead. That phone always works for me when I ring the Exchange.'

(In a deep voice: Hullo, Kenyon. The hot line to Moscow please or I'll press Button A and blast you sky high.' Burst a blown-up paper bag over the mouthpiece. Or in a falsetto: 'Hullo, Kenyon. This is Flora Bundi of Opera for the Squares.' Follow with an ear-piercing screech into the cone. There are numerous variations on the theme and dozens of voices of different kinds, Miss Clapp recoiling with shattered nerves, unprepared, because Normie strikes at any hour. A fellow has to do something with his time.)

'The phone always works for me.'

6

Outside, he looked up and down and waddled into the phone box and dialled 04. 'Number please,' said a voice from forty miles away. It was the voice of a man.

Normie felt suddenly mad, suddenly justified, suddenly vindictive. A violent nerve fluttered in his chest, his fingers snatched through the cord and tore it from the cabinet. 'If that's the way they want it,' he hissed, 'that's the way they can have it. Now they've *got* to go to Kenyon. Goodbye!'

He stuffed the cord and handset into his shirt, crossed the street, and disappeared behind the shell of Miss Beard's Haberdashery Shop, empty for thirty-five years. He tossed the pieces of telephone into the goat-eaten scrub and leant against the rotten old wall in the narrow strip of shade, overwhelmed by conscience, but positively refusing to cry.

'I've done a terrible thing. What got into me? I must have been crazy.'

He slid to the ground and sat there, hot and sweaty, in extreme discomfort, head in hands, legs in the sun.

'What a *stupid* thing to do. Now we can't ring anyone. Now we're all alone. They can't even ring back, when they get to Kenyon, to tell us what to do. Strike me, they'll kill me. One guess and they'll know it was me.'

A stick snapped and he jerked up his head with startled nerves, breath catching in his throat. Leah was there. She could have caught him so easily with his pants down inspecting his wounds.

'Oh, crumbs,' he groaned, but not aloud. She must have seen something or she wouldn't be there. Leah, of all the people in the world, peering through net curtains, looking round corners, spying like an old maid. Every thought emptied out of him, but he tried to stare back at her, tried to assume innocence.

'I saw you break the phone,' she said.

Normie turned his head away, feeling trapped.

'I understand,' she said, and to his intense surprise sat beside him, careless of dirt or her clothes, in the way that Cherry might have done, so close he could feel her shoulder there. He swayed away as though contact with Leah was forbidden, but was drawn back to her, almost against his will, until his shoulder was hard against hers (troubling him).

'We've got to stick together, Normie,' she said. 'I don't know that you were right, but I do understand.'

He glanced quickly at her, sideways, and instantly felt strange. She looked nothing like Cherry in a playful mood, Cherry teasing him, Cherry bright with fun. Leah was pale, almost as rigid as stone, and probably didn't know that his shoulder was there. No other meanings with Leah. She could be thinking only of Pan Pacific poised at the gates of the town.

'Yeh,' he said, 'we've got to pull together.'

Normie felt suddenly that he had grown.

'You broke a phone,' she said, 'so did I. You threw yourself on the road; I did, too. Did you hurt yourself when you threw yourself down? Is that why you're walking in a funny way?'

He became troubled again by her shoulder. She must have known they were close together, side by side. Was she waiting for him to hold her hand to unite them in a special way against the foe? Leah was deep though she wasn't very clever at school; you never knew what was on her mind. You were never sure whether a joke would bring a smile or send her away. It was a bit of a shock to learn that her shoulder could be warm; he'd half expected it to be cold. He glanced at her again, but she was still like stone, not looking at him, staring at the ground. He heard her father's van across the road backing up the lane. He heard another sound from another direction, Mrs Cooper's yodel for Cherry to come home. 'Strike me, Cherry,' he thought. 'What am I doing here?' A tremble inside him grew; he didn't know about Leah; he couldn't completely believe that she was there; you never confided in her; you never told her things or shared; the only safe place with Leah was to leave her on the outside. He realized that for the first time he had found a frame for his feelings about Leah. Other kids must have felt the same. You left her out because she was never really there. Anyway, she chewed her nails.

Yeh, he had grown so much in the last minute or two that he could break deliberately the touch of a girl's shoulder against his own and stand in a casual way. (Was she trying to muscle in on Cherry? Leah Elliot? Miss Purity MacPure. That Holy Jane?) 'Na,' he said, 'didn't hurt myself. Just scratched me bum sliding down the Slag. You're not going to tell about the phone?'

She shook her head but didn't look at him, because she couldn't look at him, because he had crushed her brutally and didn't care.

'We've got to stick together,' he said.

When finally she did look up it was because she knew he had gone. She put a hand to her shoulder and shivered.

Voices called from up the road. 'Hey, Stan Baxter. This barrowload of muck in the middle of the street. Is it for my lettuce bed? We'd better not leave it here.'

'It's yours, Albert, if you want it, but what good is it now?'

A third of a mile away, more or less, Shane was caught between the fear of discovery and the urge to run. To run like mad for home, shouting, 'Hey, hey. Do you know what? Do you know why they're still out there? Do you know why they haven't driven in?'

He hid among the tussocks, so close to the head of the Pan Pacific convoy that he could hear almost every word they said; too close, in fact, to get away as secretly as he had come. It was like eavesdropping, lying there, like listening through a wall. Maybe they wouldn't hurt him if they found out, but it mattered to Shane, very much, what people thought. Eavesdropping was sneaky; showing yourself was the mark of a man. Perhaps he should stand up deliberately and say, 'I heard you. Now I'm going home to tell.' Then run. That way he would be fighting in the open. It didn't matter how dirty Pan Pacific fought; that didn't count. You fought clean because of yourself, because fighting clean was right, because if you weren't right you never really won. Who said that? Auntie Sadie? No one else he knew would have thought of such a thing.

But he couldn't move because his instinct was to lie still; there might have been danger of a physical kind. Lying still, caked in dust, worried by flies, and troubled, really troubled, by the intensity of the heat. But he knew from games (sometimes still played with the little kids) that the person in hiding in grass stayed hidden only for as long as he didn't move a limb.

The fellow who lay doggo, pale skin tucked out of sight, was the last to be caught. Shane didn't want to be caught. Pan Pacific had some tough men with hard voices and hard thoughts, and the tough men were stronger than the rest. But now even the nice men were going on into town to knock it flat. ('You're under contract, you men. We stick to our end of it and you stick to yours, or else. Break a contract with us and it's a long walk back.') What would happen to a kid on his own trying to run ahead of people like that?

He'd rush up Main Street, yelling, 'Hey, do you know what? They didn't know we lived here, not any of them, except the bloke in charge, old Gibbs, cunning old fox. He'd told them it was a ghost town, heaps of stones and worm-eaten wood. What do you know, Normie! You scared 'em; yes you did! They couldn't go knocking over people's houses, some of them said, when people hadn't anywhere else to live. Knocking over a town, a real pretty old town, and digging it up, was about as dirty as you could get. What about the women and kids? they said. You should have heard the language. Talk about sunsets going down red. Auntie Sadie would've dropped dead.'

But crawling back to town was not like creeping out. Coming out he had been going ahead through scrub and from tussock to tussock towards men whose attention had been given to argument. The argument was over and now as a group they were going in.

'If trouble starts we're not pulling punches,' Gibbs said. 'No one expects that we should. These characters aren't worth your sympathy, no-hopers every one of them, living on charity, bleeding the country white. Every sweet little lurk that's going and they're in it. Don't go falling for the sob stuff. They've been turning it on for fifty years. Houses, you call them? The Company hasn't had the gall to charge them above two dollars a week rent. Would you ask a woman to live in a place like this? Would you bring up your kids in this sort of squalor? It's pre-twentieth century; it's primitive; it shouldn't exist in a country like this. No one's saying that Pan Pacific's in it for the good of their health, but we'll be doing these people a service by emptying them out. Neck and crop.'

Shane wanted to show himself, to shout defiance, to tell them the truth of a thousand beautiful things, but somehow he couldn't get up. Gibbs' voice was so strong; in another day, another age, he'd have cracked a whip.

'We could stop here,' Gibbs said, 'on this side of town and set up camp. But we won't. Stop here, and those characters will think they've won a point. We're going through, right through, in a solid block. I'll be in front. Pull over where the road widens and let me through. I go first down Main Street. If there's trouble I handle it. If we stop keep your mouths shut. No fraternizing; no getting pally with the kids. Then we camp on the other side. Where we camp makes no difference to us until we've cleaned up the site. In the long term we'll be miles out. There's a great hole out there, anyway, handy for tipping these acres of junk, if we don't set a match to it to sterilize it first. This is my project, get that straight, and it's big, and I build it my way from the ground up, from a nice clean start.'

'Go away,' Shane sobbed, 'you rotten lot.'

Bill Elliot and his van-load of men left through the back of town heading for the stock route. It added twelve miles to the run to Kenyon, would take them out past the Devil's Kitchen and Garrett's, and back across country. Bill Elliot had customers out that way, two out-stations on the Garrett property, old Dad Murphy in his little hut, shearers in season, well-sinkers, geologists (now everyone knew why those particular fellows had been roving about), and other contractors who came and went. Even Garrett himself. Bill Elliot could find his way across trackless wastes. He could sense a compass point like a pigeon in flight.

On the way out Owen Cooper spotted his daughter sitting on the ottoman under the shade of Auntie Sadie's verandah. Bill Elliot slowed the van and Owen gave a shout. 'Cherry. You're to go home. We've been calling. Didn't you hear? Your mother needs help.'

It was difficult for Cherry to stir herself. Out of common courtesy she had sat there for too long, had waited too long, had become heavy-headed. Even her curiosity came too late. 'Dad,' she called, forcing herself to her feet, 'where are you going?'

But the van had not stopped. It had taken the curve of the road
that skirted the foot of the hillock and vanished in a tunnel
of pines.

'That van was full of men. Surely they haven't left us on
our own?'

She limped to the screen door, but realized her limp was put
on. If perching there had dulled her senses it had also mended
her ache, which slightly disconcerted her. She could hardly
chew Shane's head off if nothing hurt. 'Miss Stevenson,' she
murmured into the inner gloom, almost afraid to raise her
voice, 'I've got to go home.' She listened intently. There was no
response of any kind, not even from Jack.

Really and truly, it was a bit thick. When Chinaman's Reef
needed Auntie Sadie most she had gone into a trance or got the
sulks. After all, there was the question of responsibility, something she was always ramming down other people's throats. She
had a financial interest in the Company; everyone knew she
was filthy rich.

Everyone said she had lived her peculiar kind of life only as
an act of conscience to make amends for her father's guilt.
Perhaps people didn't say it often, but everyone knew, even the
kids. Her father had been manager of the mine way back in the
days of the flood, and ever since she had lived alone in his house.
On Easter Day, 1919, with forty-three men dead, someone had
smeared a cross on the door in blood. Faintly, a mark was still
there—at least, that was what people said; and they added that,
for reasons best known to herself, Auntie Sadie had never
scrubbed it off.

'Miss Stevenson! Are you there?'

The silence worried Cherry. The least she had expected was a
growl from Jack.

'*Miss Stevenson!*' But the silence in there was all but absolute;
only the clock wheezing back and forth. Had it been the clock
all the time, not Jack?

Impulsively, angrily, recklessly (yet half afraid that something was wrong), she pushed on the door and marched into the
house, a liberty she had never taken in quite that way in her life.
'Miss Stevenson!' Then she marched from room to room, the
length of the passage, ready to leap for the ceiling if Jack came

snapping at her shins, peering into room after room, demanding a response, but getting none. 'You're in it with them,' her inner voice accused the old lady, 'aren't you? You don't care, do you? Not a jot. It's all a big act.'

The house was empty; Cherry stood on the back porch in the midst of a perfumed, steamy jungle of exotic potted plants. 'Hey,' she said. 'Hey what?' Auntie Sadie was not at home, of that there was no doubt, or Jack would have had the hem of her dress between his teeth.

One door remained; she kicked it open. Below her on the flat lay the old railway yards and the signal box; farther off still a dust cloud marked the route of departure of the Elliot van. Out there, too, was the foot track across the plain to the Devil's Kitchen and Garrett's. And there, in the chest-high scrub, was a curious moving object, shining black, reflecting the sun. It was Auntie Sadie's umbrella. She had gone with Jack out the back way, gone far beyond earshot, got away so quietly that Cherry had heard not a thing. She was stunned.

'Why, you crummy old woman . . .

'All that time I've sat out there. All that time thinking you were praying to God . . . Even thinking you might be dead . . .'

Cherry stalked back through the house and down the path to the road, deliberately mincing her hips, slamming the gate, only to stop suddenly. Sound, like distant rolling thunder, confronted her as if physically face to face; the sound of engines, big engines, many of them firing almost simultaneously into life.

She glanced bitterly back to the Stevenson house. 'They're coming,' she shrilled, 'do you hear that? Ain't it just great . . .

'*Dad.* Come back! What are you doing going away? Dad, come back!'

Cherry ran for home shouting, 'Are they coming? Are they really coming to dig us up? Normie, Normie, your gun. We'll hold them off!'

CHAPTER EIGHT

Confrontation

GOD didn't seem to be telling Shane anything. 'You tell me how to stop them, God,' Shane had said, 'and I'll do it.' Pan Pacific were doing all the telling and all the doing. God was somewhere else making new stars, spinning new galaxies for fun.

Shane huddled in the grass, assailed by noise and rattle and an awful sense of helplessness. It was like standing on top of the Slag again, watching that horrible army coming closer, but worse, because now they were only yards away, crunching and rumbling past him. He huddled there in the way of cowering boys of other years and other places hiding in ditches and hedgerows, bewildered by mechanized divisions overrunning their countries, shelling their houses, killing their brothers. 'It's not fair, the big bullies.' Shane found himself on his feet, weeping, and suddenly running like a frightened animal, caught in a maze of vegetation that seemed higher and denser than it had any right to be.

'Stop that kid.'

'After him.'

But Shane's dizzy escape became a fall that he could not recover from. He hit the earth hard and lay there with his heartbeat shaking him, sweat breaking out like a rash, but the voices did not approach. No hand seized him. The rattle and rumble bore on, paying no attention. When he looked up, when he swayed on his feet blinking through mists, the road was not where he expected to find it, but behind him, surprisingly distant, and a big saloon car drawing a caravan was lurching along the roadside near the town slowly overtaking the others, horn blowing. If there had been voices they had been in his mind. They had not seen him or had not cared. Miserably, he knew he had been pushed aside as an object of no importance.

'I live here. I don't want to go away. Why should I have to? Why are their rights better than mine?'

He felt smaller and smaller while the world grew larger—and Pan Pacific owned the lot.

They were stirring up dust again from the edges. Red lights and white lights were flashing. 'We live here now,' the lights said, 'all the rights we want we've got. We've got the title deeds, kid.' They were in a solid block, crawling, as if next Christmas was time enough, with only a few feet between them, smothering the earth. Two miles of convoy had closed up, but had not shrunk. Why didn't the road sink? Solid for hundreds of yards, a solid block, machinery massed, bulldozers and front-end loaders, tankers, cranes and power-shovels, clattering trucks, compressors and generators, caravans and trailers, tall blank-sided vehicles that might have been workshops or kitchens or refrigerated transports or cages for monsters with mouths like caverns. On wheels a million dollars; easily a million dollars in iron-clad ranks; each dollar to hammer Chinaman's Reef flat.

Shane felt smaller still while big things became bigger and the Powers that didn't care spread past the ends of the earth.

'Didn't you hear me, God, or is God really somewhere else? What sort of slop is it she's fed us all these years about God caring? I know you don't care, or thousands of kids wouldn't die sick, earthquakes wouldn't happen, volcanoes wouldn't blow up. A fella can't fight clean, you know that. This mob doesn't know what clean is. *You* can't fight 'em either, because they're here and you're not. You're too busy with important things like singin' Hallelujahs to yourself.'

Normie, by stealth, had taken possession of the lean-to bath-room on the end of the verandah at the side of the house, with the door on the catch. Door of planks painted green, sheet iron ceiling of corrugated pink, casement window of dimpled glass, yellow bath on clawed tin feet, and oppressive heat. Normie's was a nerve-racking business of furious activity and breathless halts, repairing himself, because Mum was in and out of the house, rushing back and forth, thudding past the bathroom door every time she plunged in or out. An awfully tricky business patching parts of your body that were out of sight, standing on your ear sponging and dusting with talc, every instant expecting the door to shake to Mum's assault. Underpants stuffed in the bath heater, buried under newspaper and sticks emptied out of the drum ready for next bath night.

Mum's composure had fallen apart. Mum in a panic could never stand still, was like a human elephant shaking the place, not seeing straight, talking non-stop, hearing clearly only her own voice, a mighty dangerous mountain of flesh. 'Those men are thoughtless,' she ranted. 'One of them should have stayed back. A town full of helpless women and not a man in sight.'

If Mum had sat on Pan Pacific she'd have squashed them flat.

'Normie, where are you? Where has that boy gone? Clara, have you seen your brother? I want that boy back. Maureen, find your brother. The last thing his father said, "Hold him down. Lock him up. Don't let him out of your sight. I wouldn't trust him as far as I could spit." '

Strangers thought Mum was placid, but they only knew her when she was 'out'.

'Normeee! Normeee!'

Clara and Maureen panicking about like frightened sheep. 'They're coming, Mum.' 'Bloomin' old Normie's gone into smoke.' 'Where will we hide, Mum?' 'Will they knock us over now, Mum, or have their lunch first?'

'Normeee! Normeee!'

Normie in a tangle with sticking plaster, sticking like fury, like fighting an octopus. All he wanted to do was shriek but didn't dare squeak.

Someone else was panting outside, stumbling over the step, banging on the wall. 'Normie, are you there?' Strike a fellow pink. Now Cherry had come, adding her yell to all the rest. 'Normie, your gun!'

'Gun? Gun? Has that boy taken his gun?'

Thud. Thud. Out came Mum with a body rush. 'Oh, my God. He hasn't got his gun. Oh, my God. Murder's the only thing he's never done. Normeeeee! Bring back that gun. Oh, Cherry, bless your heart. Is there time to stop him if we run? Oh, my God, the heat. Don't stand there dumb-struck, love; which way has he gone?'

Thud. Thud. Mum over the step, heading for the street, bellowing, 'Normeee, Normeee.' Clara wailing like a silly parrot, 'Normie's got his gun.' Mum yelling, 'Normie, bring back that gun.' Mum yelling again, 'Rose, Rose. Madge, Madge. Did you see him? That young savage has taken his gun.'

Normie drenched in sweat, plastered with talc, trying to drag on his pants, staggering on one foot. Cherry only inches away beyond the door making noises like she'd been hit on the head. Normie panting, 'It'd be funny if it wasn't horrible.'

Voices farther off like shrill reeds heard over drums: 'Normie Muir, don't you shoot.'

'Cherry came from the Stevenson house. I saw her running down.'

'Stop the convoy. Don't let it through. There'll be bloodshed. We've got to find that kid.'

'Where'd Cherry go? She must know where he is.'

The crazy lot.

Normie bursting out of the bathroom, stuffing in his shirt, almost frightening Cherry sick. 'Strike me, Cherry, are you nuts? Why didn't you stop her before she went berserk? She'll never believe now I didn't have the gun.'

But Cherry's cheeks were taut again; she was the wild one at heart. 'What were you doing in there?'

'Changin' me pants.'

'You've got the same ones on.'

'I was changing them!'

'Why didn't you stop her yourself?'

'With no pants on?'

Cherry took a breath. She was minutes ahead of him. 'You *have* got your gun. Can't you see what it's done? Let's get it quick and duck out the back.'

Leah was drawn to the road in fright, drawn out against her will as if reluctant to show her face, as if the security of her particular sadness lay behind Miss Beard's Haberdashery Shop. But the curiosity of fright drew her out, edging along the side wall and on to the open street, leaving her stark and exposed between fear and force. They had been calling for Normie, they had been calling for Cherry, they had called even for Shane, but not for her. They never counted her in. 'Why didn't you call for me?' she asked, but how could they hear?

Normie on the loose with a gun. A gun for Christmas—what a crazy thought.

'It's against the law,' Dad had said. 'The Muirs have got me tossed. He's too young. He's too silly. He'll blow off someone's head. But for a lad he's a wonderful shot.'

'Why did you sell it to them, Dad, if you knew all along it was Normie who'd get it?'

There were little kids everywhere, darting about. 'Normie, Normie,' they were yelling. And the women were rushing from tree to tree, peering up. 'Normie, you mustn't shoot.'

Pan Pacific was creeping in from the other end. Enormous Pan Pacific. How could it be so big? So long, it was out of sight. So tall, the leaves of trees were plucked and tossed as it approached. Pan Pacific was creeping in as though testing the water, first a toe, then a foot, then surging in, clanking, rumbling, rattling, squirting black oil smoke, shedding dust from its flanks.

Normie with a gun. You stop them, Normie; you stop them with that gun. It's your line of business, Normie; Shane couldn't pull a trigger to save his life. Build yourself a fortress, Normie; don't let any of them scare you off.

'Leah. Leah Elliot.'

They were counting her in; they were calling from a distance with all the power of Mrs Muir's mass. 'Don't stand there, love. Run to stop them. There'll be bloodshed.' Mrs Muir's arm went up in command like a finger-post. 'They mustn't get to this end of the street.'

But she didn't want to run. They only counted her in when their wishes were different from her own. She wanted Normie to fire his gun, but hardly ever put her own wants first. She ran because it was her nature to obey.

Leah ran towards the flashing lights with her girlish, fragile, dainty run, towards the dust and black oil smoke and half-seen shapes and she seemed to have lived the experience before, the hurt and loneliness and the weight of the world, and suddenly it *was* her wish and had nothing to do with anyone else. It was her wish to live it through to the end and stop them with her body offered as a sacrifice. She saw the man's eyes behind the windscreen, and his grey hair, she heard the shattering horn blast that seemed to issue from his open mouth, and somehow it went wrong as it always did and she was beating with her open hand on the car, on the driver's side, yelling back at the horn, 'You've got to stop. Stop, I say. Stop! There's a boy with a gun.'

Then she was running beside the car, still banging with her hand. 'Do you want to be shot? Wind the window down. Listen to me. Why have you got the window up on a day like this? Stop, stop. You've just got to stop.' But the car was going faster and she could hardly keep up and horns behind her were blowing to frighten her away, overwhelming her voice, and the man with the grey hair looked only ahead, ignoring her presence as he might ignore a dog.

She couldn't hold the pace, and the sound of horns blasted her into the gutter as it was meant they should, but she shouted for as long as she had breath, 'Oh stop. Do stop.' Vehicle by vehicle they overtook her, metal monsters that had nothing to do with her idea of grown-up men, until she couldn't even stumble. 'All right,' she groaned, 'get shot.'

Her energy collapsed but remnants of pride held her to her feet. There was shade where she was, a tree overhanging, tossing, as high vehicles scraped through its arch, leaves and twigs showering her, fumes and smell, and the heads of men in profile parading past, each intent upon the vehicle immediately in front, ignoring her, as the grey-haired man had ignored her— or were they all too ashamed to look? Rushing on into the sights of Normie's gun, doing exactly as she wished, but only because they thought she wanted them to stop.

'All right. Get shot.'

They filled Chinaman's Reef from south to north. There was nothing of Main Street left. They filled it with their nightmarish noise and their overflowing hugeness and what was Normie's cheap little gun against something like that? They wouldn't even hear the shot. His silly little bullet would bounce off. There should have been a law against people like Pan Pacific. You were equal only if you were rich.

Suddenly brake lights flared red and brake drums squealed

with dust. Mammoth machines rocked on low-loaders brought
abruptly to a halt. There was a crunching impact somewhere
farther back. Back there at least one driver had overrun his
mark, and up front there was an unbelievable event: the leading
car was in the ditch, angled sharply to the road, with the women
of Chinaman's Reef wrenching at doors that were apparently
locked.

Normie saw his mother do it and he didn't believe it. A freak
of timing opened for him a narrow angle of sight like a ray on
Auntie Sadie's end of town. Running low with Cherry, breaking
out with the gun along wire back fences where there used to be a
street, he saw his mother beyond tree-trunks and gaps in bushes
and the walls of empty houses, as though he had glimpsed her
through a shaft of light. There she was with a lump of rock.

But Normie was still running hard, stooping with the gun like
a soldier in a newsreel, bent on overtaking the convoy, on somehow getting out in front, and there was nothing to see except
walls and wire fences and goat-eaten bushes and tree-trunks and
tussocks, and suddenly Cherry was almost under his feet, Cherry
with a wide-eyed look. 'Normie, what was that?'

He was confused and short of breath and already certain that
he had not seen through to the street, had not seen his mother,
and could not have seen her extraordinary act.

'Pan Pacific's stopped,' Cherry said. 'Did you hear a crash?'

So Normie said it, but still didn't believe it: 'My Mum threw
a rock.' And every word was like a trumpet note.

Cherry stared. 'Your Mum? Throw a rock? You're joking.
She's belted *you* for doing less.'

Normie went quickly back, retracing his steps. 'I saw her,'
he said.

'You dreamt it.'

'I saw her through a gap.'

'What gap? There's no gap.'

But there was, just like a shaft or a ray as Normie had seen it,
with a stainless steel caravan all of twenty feet long at the end of
it and the back of a car that must have run into the ditch.

'I did see it,' Normie said. 'Look.'

'But you said your Mum.'

'She was *there*.'

Across the lane of their sight Cherry saw a small boy run off (Was it Peter? She didn't know), and Normie saw a man he had seen before, that fellow with the bald head and the sun-glasses and the nasty disposition. He came barging in as if he was heading for a fight. 'Golly, Cherry, what's up?'

'Your Mum's not there, Normie.'

'She was! She threw a rock.' He was shocked. 'Why would she do a thing like that?'

'Why would we fire a shot?'

He looked at her, puzzled by the changed tone of voice. 'But a rock. She aimed it at the windscreen. A dirty great lump of rock!'

'So what? They're asking for it, aren't they?' A peculiar excitement was gripping Cherry. 'Since when have you squibbed a fight?'

Normie stepped back from her a pace. 'But I wouldn't hurt anyone. You know I wouldn't do that. Punchin' some kid up the snout has got nothing to do with firing that kind of shot.'

'You're yellow.'

His gun felt horrible to the touch, as if possession of it at that time and place meant that someone was already lying with a bullet in the neck. He dropped it and stepped back another pace, all mixed up. 'What am I doing with it? What'd you talk me into this for? I coulda killed someone. . . . Holy cow, and Mum gets in such a flap. Has she gone and done just that?'

He backed away again and came up hard against a fence and looked anxiously to the street, but the street had gone, the angle of sight had changed. They were as private from that tormented world as if it had been miles away.

Cherry stooped and picked up his gun. 'Come on,' she said, 'don't get soft.'

'No, Cherry, we can't do it.'

'They're asking for it. What have they done to us?'

'Dad said we couldn't stop them! I heard him, Cherry. I heard him say it. They're in the right.'

'If they're in the right I'd hate to be around when they're wrong.' She pushed the butt into his chest. 'Are you a man or a mouse?'

Men were running both ways on the street, a few had headed

for the crash farther back, others had gone forward to the car in the ditch. They were shouting back and forth over engines not yet switched off and Leah was somewhere in the middle.

'Out of the way, kid, or you'll get hurt.'

'It's a rum sort of joint, all right.'

'Is he injured? Is he bad?'

'Gibbs! There'll be a howl about this.'

'Was there a shot?'

'Some stupid woman with a rock.'

'Blood all over his face. They've had to smash a window to get the door unlocked.'

'There's some damage back there that'll cost a mint to fix.'

'Talk about the Wild West.'

Two of them went past with long spanners in their hands; one tore a picket from the Muir's front fence. Leah couldn't even think. 'I told you,' she shrilled, 'I told you you'd get shot and you wouldn't stop.'

'Go home, girl, or you'll be getting hurt.'

But she stumbled along the footpath, shouting at them, 'Leave us alone. You've got no right.'

'It's a bunch of crazy women. There's not a man about.'

'What do you do with women? They're as savage as cats.'

'You'll get shot,' Leah shrilled.

Shane cut for the road across the flats, running as hard as he could, hearing the crash in his mind over and over again, feverishly wanting to know why, that beautiful, beautiful crash, imagining that someone had felled a tree across the street or attacked them with another vehicle from the front. Old Dad Murphy with his horse and cart? He wouldn't give way for an avalanche. How else could they bring Pan Pacific up sharp? How else? And it had ground to a horrible halt, its tail stuck out of Main Street like a spear driven in to the end of its shaft. Was it Normie being mad again or one of the men? Whose father would take such a drastic step? No one's father; not one of them was violent enough. Mr Muir had been a tough egg once; you'd never guess it now; butter wouldn't melt in his mouth.

But Pan Pacific was *stopped*. Stopped in Mr Gibbs' solid block!

Stopped and sewn up in Main Street, maybe outside Auntie Sadie's gate! Stopped by witchcraft. Stopped by a spell. By a road turned suddenly into a pit. By legions of demons rushing up. Haaa, Mr Gibbs, you've copped your little lot. Someone's stopped you and someone's piled up, or there wouldn't have been a crash.

Shane reached the road where the peppercorns began behind the hall, short on breath and light in the head. He drooped there for a pause of seconds, shaken by his own pulse, and ran on again to the verandah of the Pride of Ballydoon and clung to a post, physically distressed. Oh, it wasn't like Chinaman's, it was like somewhere else, like a city lane all snarled in traffic and brute force, where everyone hated each other on sight, and an enormous vehicle had rammed another and all but dislodged from itself a compressor or a generator as big as a roadroller. It teetered with a list on the edge of the low-loader while men stood back, perhaps at a loss, and others hurriedly laid out ropes and props. 'Serves you right,' Shane groaned, 'I hope it falls off. Go on, somebody, give it a push. If you don't do it, I'll push it myself.'

But they had no thought for him there and he straightened up against the post, remembering a railing he had seen that morning hanging from a second-floor balcony round the side up top.

A face Leah knew, all pale and set, came out of the confusion of the street. Oh, it was a wonderful sight.

'Mum.'

'Leah,' her mother said, 'I'd have done anything to spare you from this. You should be home behind locked doors. We've sent all the little ones off. Mrs Muir threw a stone and hit him in the head. But he wouldn't stop. The silly man wouldn't stop.'

Then Leah was swept along at her mother's pace, holding her tightly by the hand, heading back down the street. 'I hope Miss Clapp answers this time. For her sake and for ours. Goodness knows what we'll do if she won't. He wouldn't stop for Mrs Muir. He wouldn't stop. It's a fractured skull, I suppose, or concussion at least. The silly, silly man. She only did it so he wouldn't get shot. The trouble that Normie causes. She only did it, poor woman, to protect Normie from himself. "Stop, stop," she was crying, "or my boy might shoot." The arrogance of the fellow driving on like that.'

A truculent young man with a picket in his hand suddenly stood in their path. 'Hey, Missus. Did you throw that rock?'

Mrs Elliot continued walking against a sudden tug, dragging Leah with her. 'I wouldn't discuss it with you,' she said, 'if I had.' And collided with him, kicking his shin with an iron-sharp toe.

'Mum,' Leah cried out.

The young man reeled backwards, hopping on one foot, yelping, and Mrs Elliot marched on, astonished at her own audacity. 'Use that picket,' she shouted over her shoulder, 'or any more of that language and I wouldn't be surprised if you got shot.' Then she stopped, because her voice had carried and echoed back. Engines had not drowned it. Every engine had been switched off.

Leah shook at her side, appalled by her mother's foolhardiness. They were so close to the Store, only a few steps more and they'd be safe, but she had stopped. And there were so many men and the feeling was ugly. Her mother was a timid woman who hardly ever raised her voice.

'Did you hear me,' she shouted, and her voice was almost coarse, 'or do I say it again? You'll get shot. There's a boy with a rifle and he's as hot-headed as they come. If you men are thinking rough you'd better think twice. He's in a high place with the street in his sights. That boy can shoot. He could hit a rabbit at fifty yards when he was ten. Why do you think his mother threw the rock? To save that stupid man from getting shot. Now I'm ringing for the doctor and I don't give a tinker's curse how many of you he's got to patch up. It's a long drive out, so make his trip worthwhile. Go ahead, get rough and get shot.'

The trembling woman saw not a single face, fixed her eyes on nothing and simply shouted while her heart raced, then pulled Leah, who could scarcely stand, into the illusion of security in the telephone box. She crushed in, dragged the door shut and was almost ill from the heat there and from the violence of her own reactions to herself. 'Oh, Leah,' she whimpered, 'what have

I done, what have I done?' Her hands were visibly shaking and she was deathly white.

'You were marvellous, Mum.'

'I was terrified, love.' She started crying.

'Don't let them see you cry, Mum. You were marvellous. You scared them stiff.'

'It's no use, dear, I'm not made for it. It's all too much. Oh, I wish your father hadn't gone.'

'You were marvellous, Mum. Don't spoil it. Don't cry.'

She was past reason or argument or comfort. 'Ring up for me, Leah. I'll never, never find the voice.'

Then Leah remembered what Normie had done to the telephone and tried to hide it with her hand making it all the more apparent.

'Ring up for me, Leah. Quickly. The heat in here is too much. I think I'll faint.'

'All right, Mum, I'll ring up.' She tried to force her mother out but the woman wouldn't budge. 'You go into the shop, Mum; go on.'

'How can I leave you here, child, with all these men? A mother can't do that.'

'Of course you can, Mum.' The phone was so obvious it was a miracle she didn't see it. She was *looking* at it. 'They wouldn't hurt me, Mum. Not now, after what you've said. Normie will take care of us with his gun.'

The woman drew herself up and actually opened the door about an inch. 'Yes,' she said, 'I believe that and it terrifies me. Whatever will we do if he fires a shot—and kills somebody? It'll be my fault.'

'If Normie heard, Mum, he'll understand. He's not as silly as that. He'll shoot to miss.' (Why wouldn't she go? Why wouldn't she go?)

'And then perhaps hit someone else, even one of us.' But she pushed out of the box, across the footpath, and into the shop. And Leah slumped against the shelf and her stomach was in knots, slumped there and moaned, 'What now? What next? There's only half a phone. And that man's lying up there hit on the head.'

She was moaning and hardly knowing it, but was aware of

men. Men outside with folded arms and broad shoulders
exchanging comments, one walking away, but three too close,
almost too close to be deceived, men big enough to take the
telephone box apart with their bare hands, squinting at her
with frowning brows. The men she was used to were not like
these. She only knew the men who lived in Chinaman's Reef
and round about, only knew her schoolmasters, and the bus
driver, and one uncle whose face she scarcely remembered.
Strangers were a different race.

It was a street full of huge machines, of masses of metal, of a
crowding presence. A street full of threat. Chinaman's Reef had
gone crazy. She felt like a creature in a pit, caught, but was
fumbling clumsily with the directory, turning over pages, pretending to look for the number, even pretending to dial
Kenyon, leaning into the corner behind notices stuck to the
windows with her hand to her ear, desperately pretending. 'Oh,
Normie,' she moaned, 'fire a shot or do something silly. Distract
their attention.' Pretending, with eyes outside watching her
lips, and ears listening for the murmur of her voice.

'Is that you, Doctor? Oh, hullo, Doctor. Oh, it's not. So
you're out playing golf. Will you take a message when you come
back? There's a man in an accident. Yes, hit on the head. Yes,
they say he's unconscious. Mrs Cooper's looking after him; I
suppose it's Mrs Cooper; she always patches us up when we get
hurt. Mrs Baxter's gone for hot water, well she would, I suppose,
or else she's gone home to dress. She had her dressing-gown on;
of course she usually does. You see her in the afternoon sometimes, still not dressed. Mrs Muir's sitting in the gutter, crying I
think. She's in a panic, she really is. I hope they believe I'm
talking to you, Doctor, or are you still out at golf? Oh, I hope
they believe me because what will happen to me if they
don't?'

She banged her hand on the hook to make the bell tingle and
groaned against the bench, breathless from heat and fright,
afraid to look up, afraid to go out.

Shane leapt for the railing hanging from the balcony at the side
of Ballydoon, leapt several times with all the strength he could

summon before it came down with a crack, shedding blisters of brown paint and bone-dry splinters and the smell of oregon dust. Poor old Ballydoon; another rib gone. 'But I'm not going to burn you,' Shane panted, 'not this time for the fire, this time to show them who's what.' It was long like a caber, a twelve-foot extension of his reach, twelve feet of oregon three inches square, bevelled at the edges by the hand of a tradesman in 1891. 'Did you think it would be used for this?'

Yeh. He'd run across the road and up their blind side. Two vehicles to pass before he'd be close enough. Then he'd get the railing up over his head, he'd get it up or bust, then charge. 'Hey, kid,' they'd yell, 'what are you doing with that wood?' 'Cooking your goose,' he'd bellow and pitch it true and straight with all his might at the leaning machine, striking it near the top. Over it would go. Down it would crash. Bits and pieces on the road. Then he'd run, shouting back, 'How do you like your own medicine, you rotten lot? Here's one kid you won't be fraternizing with.'

Shane dragged his lump of wood behind him, bumping it over the cobbles, along the lane to the street.

'Then they'll be trapped. Auntie Sadie will have blocked them off at her end and I'll have blocked them off at this. Mr Gibbs and his solid blooming block. Start a panic and they'll be piling up everywhere trying to get out.'

Then he was running, dragging grimly on his length of wood, on to the street as he had planned to do, bumping it across the drainage ditch with a bone-jarring jolt, losing control of it, losing it completely. It struck him under the armpit and knocked him from his feet. But Shane scrambled up and grabbed his wood again, blindly intent upon his purpose. Then he heard a penetrating voice. 'That's the spirit, lad. Here, I'll take it. We could use a few lengths like that. It's good meeting one of you not bent on cutting our throats.'

Shane saw the man pacing towards him, then saw others, blurred in a background. It was like opening a door and finding a crowd when you'd expected an empty room. It caught him by surprise and he went blank.

'Did you hurt yourself, lad?'

Shane numbly shook his head.

'If that machine slips,' the man said, 'someone could get killed.'

He took the piece of wood and Shane let him do it. 'Thanks, lad. Couldn't be better. Bring us a few more and you'll earn yourself a dollar.' The man thrust a hand in his pocket. 'Catch,' he said, and flicked a silver coin that Shane instinctively caught. 'A little on account,' the man said and flashed a grin, but Shane sickened. 'Keep your stinking money,' he shouted and threw the coin back, viciously, missing the man but striking metal somewhere with a clang. Shane backed off with everything inside him at white heat. He saw nothing of the man's shock and heard nothing of what he said. 'I'm getting that machine, Mister.' Then he ran, two or three ways at once, and darted behind the last vehicle into a pair of thick arms that clamped on him like a vice, that smothered and terrified him. Shane bit and was suddenly free again. All he could see was the shell of the blacksmith's shop, gaping open, and he plunged for it, straight in and straight through, out the back, and this time they were really chasing him, there was nothing imaginary about it. The voice was there and so were the heavy feet. 'You bit! You animal! No one gets away with that!' A hand was there, too, snatching for his shirt, but Shane was frantic and agile and knew every inch of ground, every bush and every trick. He stopped as sharply as a rabbit, as he had done a hundred times in games, and the man blundered over the top of him and reeled full-length into a heap of broken bricks.

Shane left him there and scrambled through the fence, as wild as the animal the man had said he was, gasping from a stitch.

Leah couldn't survive in the phone box for another moment and she groped from its stifling heat into the open, leaning on the door as it closed hydraulically behind her, her weight sinking back with it. They were waiting for her. They were there; one man directly confronting her. Khaki-coloured shorts, bare legs with muscles bunched, bald head, sun-glasses, and a smile that was neither nasty nor nice.

'The doctor?' he said, leaning forward, placing an arm on either side of her, caging her, but not touching her. Leah almost panicked, but somehow held on. 'The doctor?' the man repeated. 'Can he come?'

She was struggling for her breath. 'He's out.'

'Why not ring another?'

'There's not another.'

'*No* other doctor?'

'You're lucky there's one. I've left a message. He'll come, he'll come.' She wanted to push herself from the door, to break out and run.

'You're lying.'

'There's no other doctor. There's not, there's not.'

'You could have rung the hospital. They'd have sent someone else. Now you're not going to tell me there's not a hospital.'

Leah shook her head.

'There's not?'

'There is, there is. Oh, please let me pass.'

'But you couldn't ring them, could you? Any more than you could ring the doctor on a telephone without a handset.'

Leah moaned and the man stood back. 'Mr Gibbs has a daughter,' he said, 'about your age, I think. I hope she'd treat your father, if he'd been hit with a rock, better than that.'

Leah cried, 'I live here. Don't you understand? And I asked him to stop. I ran and ran and ran, asking him to stop. He wouldn't even look at me. What sort of a man is that?' Then she turned cold, and felt as she had never felt in her life. 'Go away,' she said, 'before I slap you in the face.'

Suddenly, she pushed herself clear of the telephone box and all but butted him in the chest. He recoiled, and before he could recover himself she had crossed the footpath and stepped smartly into the shop. His hand reached the screen door but Leah had snibbed the catch.

'Sort it out yourself,' she said. 'I hope his headache lasts for a month. If the stupid man had stopped like any decent man would have done, he'd never have got hurt. He can thank his lucky stars it was only a rock.' Then she slammed the main door and was astonished by the look of her mother, still visibly shaking, placing Dad's shotgun gingerly on the counter. 'Mum,' she exclaimed, 'what are you doing with that?'

The woman was fluttery and tearful and couldn't control her

hands. 'Oh, love, I don't know, but·if he had laid a finger, a
solitary finger on you I think I'd have shot him. Oh, love,
things are in a terrible state. If I'd pulled the trigger I'd have
shot you as well. I didn't think. They're horrible things, these
guns. They spray pellets all over the place. I'd have disfigured
you for life.'

'Don't worry, Mum. Don't carry on. No harm's done. I'm
all right.'

'Oh, Leah, someone's made a terrible mistake. They should
never have come into this township in the way that they've
done. I'm afraid for the outcome. No one's thinking straight.
Oh, my darling girl, that you should be exposed to this.
Violence is a disease. It's going from one of us to the other.
We're peaceful people. We're harmless people. We don't know
what to do in situations like this. We don't know from one
moment to the next what's happening anywhere else. Oh, Leah,
I fear for the outcome. Darling, you've got to keep off the
street.'

Leah's courage was of little use; it rarely was; Mum could
usually stifle it in a minute or less. 'The phone,' she murmured,
'wouldn't work either.'

'Well . . . that's Mr Big Man's bad luck, though perhaps Miss
Clapp will feel the regret.' The woman gave an odd shiver
which possessed her for an instant from head to foot. 'Are you
hungry, love? Will we see if we can salvage some lunch?'

Someone was hammering on the door, but they left him to
hammer, the woman taking the girl by the hand and leading
her out. It was Shane, almost ready to drop, hammering and
rattling at the outside screen. 'Oh, open up. Please open up.
You're in there, I know.'

The man was still coming, doggedly to the pursuit, but walking now with a limp, deliberately walking, scratched by barbed
wire and thorns, his hair disordered, one knee and an elbow
skinned from his contact with the bricks, but walking deliberately with a hand gesturing, palm foremost, arm out-
stretched. 'He's mine. Don't anyone touch. Look at that.
He bit.'

Shane pressed to the window glass, smearing it with sweat,
banging it, peering in. 'It's me. It's Shane. Let me in.' But no

one was there to open up and Shane had to go on again, hand over hand along the window ledge and then away from its support across the open face of Elliot's lane.

'Dad! Can't you hear me? Where are you?'

There were men at a dozen points, but not one that he knew. They had turned Chinaman's Reef into a foreign place.

'It was self-defence, Mister. I didn't think. I don't bite people. Dad, Dad, it's Shane!'

There was nowhere to go. Only derelict houses and each was a trap. Only Elliot's lane and what was the use of that? Everything was a dead end, the side of a house or a machine or a man or a lane that finished at a fence. Home was farther up the street and across the other side beyond a wall of metal as high as the sky, and Normie's place was much too far to drag his feet. A fellow could get so much from himself, then nothing was left.

'Blood,' the man said. 'See that. Drawn by your teeth.'

But Shane wouldn't look. He stumbled on a few steps until he reached the next fence and leant against it, hanging on. 'Hit me, mister,' he said. 'Get it over, will you. What are you doin', following me like this?'

'He's only a pint-sized boy,' someone said, 'lay off,' and Shane hazily fixed the source of the voice. Was it the tired-looking, tall man again, first encountered when Normie had stopped the convoy about a hundred years back?

'He bit!'

'O.K., he bit. What'd you do to him?'

'Tooth marks! Tooth marks! Do you see that?'

'Sure, tooth marks, but lay off the rough stuff up this end of the street. That wild-looking kid's got himself a gun and if the rough stuff starts someone gets shot. For mine, I reckon that's fair enough. Tit for tat.'

Shane, confused, slid down the side of the fence and sat at the bottom, propped up.

'If he'd bitten you, mate, you wouldn't be so quick to his defence.'

'I'm not defending him; I'm looking after myself. We're taking that gun seriously; the kid's mother certainly is. So if you want to fight you take him back your end of the street and beat him to a pulp.'

Shane's pursuer dropped his arms to his sides, flushed with anger and embarrassment. 'Whose side are you on, mate?'

'My own side,' the tall man said, 'but I'm beginning to wonder what we're at. I reckon Gibbs got his just deserts and I reckon you belong to his club. What'd we come here for? To terrorize kids? To start a vendetta if they fight back? Go on, be your age, shove off, or I'll sool the women on to you, they'll scratch your eyes out, and God knows what the men will do to you when they get back. My opinion, *mate*, for what it's worth, is that for once in its greedy life Pan Pacific's bitten—' Shane heard the tall man choke himself off.

There was silence, a conspicuous slowing of activity along the street, then a freezing of movement and everyone looking in the same direction, silence moving outwards like concentric waves to areas beyond Shane's sight. His own consciousness seemed to be away out there fleeing from him but then it came rushing back.

'Easy, girlie,' the tall man said, stiffly, as if the words belonged to a language he hardly ever spoke. 'That thing might go off.'

Leah, a splash of white, dominated the street from the store verandah, with her back to the window, with her feet apart, with her father's shotgun supported awkwardly from the hip, and Shane struggled to grasp the meaning of what his eyes could not accept, Leah hanging on to a gun so big she could scarcely hold it up, Leah Elliot who hardly ever came to life in a public place, the girl who wouldn't say boo to a goose.

He pulled himself up and gripped the fence, wondering whether to run, wondering whether he could or should, while at the edges of his vision men were dropping out of sight, others were stepping for cover behind vehicles and tree-trunks and verandah posts, and five were stranded at close range like statues of wood—Shane's pursuer, Shane's rescuer and three others, one of them caught in the act of approach, black eyebrows starkly arched on his bald head, sun-glasses slipping on the bridge of his nose. That one man, of them all, seemed to have been struck with terror; that one man and perhaps Leah herself.

She panted through an unnaturally open mouth, tears clearly on her cheeks. The gun barrel dipped and swayed, constantly traversing a sweep, but Leah made no sound that anyone could hear. Perhaps she tried, but the nerve that had brought her on to the street might have run its course. 'Strike me dead,' groaned Shane. 'She'll kill herself.'

'Point it at the ground,' the tall man said, 'that's a dangerous weapon, get your finger off the trigger.'

Leah made no effort to speak but struggled to keep the gun up.

'It's for someone strong,' the tall man said. 'Don't use it, girlie; it's too big. You *might* hurt others, but you *will* hurt yourself.'

'Shane,' she said, in a hoarse, dry voice.

'If this is Shane, you can see he's not hurt. You're not, are you, lad?'

Shane shook his head.

'Tell her. Let her hear.'

'I'm not hurt, Leah.' But in a way it was a lie; he could scarcely croak. They heard a sound in the background, hard heels clattering on bare boards and a woman's muffled shout, 'Leah!'

'The rest of you,' Leah said shrilly, 'can go away. Get back in your motor cars and go away. You horrible people, go away.'

'Perhaps we wish we could, but it's not for us to decide things of that kind, or for you either.'

'I said get in your motor-cars and go away.'

'We can't, girlie.' The tall man's voice was hoarsening; he had never been meant to stand as spokesman for Pan Pacific. 'Even if we feel for you the road is blocked back and front. We're bottled up. We've got an injured man in a house up the street and he's the decision-maker. Look here, girlie, we'll get nowhere like this. We'll not solve our problems by threatening force.'

'Go away!'

'We *can't*, lass, unless we *walk*.'

'Well, *walk*!' Leah dragged the gun up and even Shane went to earth. She dragged it up and aimed over the housetops, recoiling against the shop window, expecting a blow like a kick from a horse, but the gun did not go off.

'Disarm her,' someone shouted.

Shane tried to lead the rush, tried frantically to get there first, but he was pushed in the back and sent reeling into the lane against the wall of the shop. He collapsed on his knees, partly stunned, sick and desperate from being knocked about. It was then that he heard the shot and a ricocheting bullet whining into silence. What that meant he could not even guess.

CHAPTER NINE

All the King's Horses

SHANE tried not to weep again, but by trying made it worse. For years he had cried so little, but this morning he had cried so much. He was so ashamed and so mixed up. This morning it was not like his own life, but someone else's life grafted unhappily on to his own. He wasn't Shane any more. He didn't know himself. When had Shane been homeless? When had adults been anything other than firm or kind or just a little bit cranky at the worst? When had Shane been thrown against buildings and chased by cursing men and terrorized by noise and overwhelmed by force? A terrible argument still assaulted him, almost physically, with its passion and its threats. Women shrilling and men shouting, people yelling about police intervention and court actions and juvenile delinquents and the rights of citizens to defend their own hearths, people yelling about things that in his world had never had a place.

Then, oddly like an afterthought, someone heaved him up and stood him on his feet.

'Don't cry, darling. Don't frighten me if you're not hurt.'

'Oh, Mum,' he sobbed, 'where have you been? Where's Dad?'

'Help yourself, darling. You're too heavy for me to hold up. Don't cry. Everything will be all right.'

'*Where's Dad?*'

'He won't be long. They'll be back soon. The men have gone to Kenyon to get Shire help. They had to do something, darling. They didn't know what to do for the best.'

He shook against her, questioning hazily a grown-up logic that would leave boys and girls to fight against men, that would set Leah Elliot up against a window-pane with a gun.

'Leah, Mum?'

'Leah's all right.'

'Someone got shot.'

'No one got shot. You're the one that's in the mess. Your clothes are ruined. You're all torn and scratched. Oh, Shane, your Sunday best.'

'I'm sorry, Mum.'

He leant against the shop wall with his right arm over his eyes, to smother his crying and to block off everything of the street. 'Mum, *the shot?*'

'Normie, darling, and Cherry I think. They can't be blamed. It's Mrs Elliot's fault; shouting it out at the top of her voice. They must be in the pines past Miss Stevenson's house.'

'Who did they hit?'

'No one, thank God. But no violence, I said, and the place has gone mad. Leah with a gun, locking her mother in the house out of the shop. Normie and Cherry sniping from the tree-tops. How can women like us handle trouble like this? And Miss Stevenson hasn't shown her face.'

He wasn't leaning any more, but was being led.

'Leah, Mum?'

'I said she's all right.'

'But, Mum, the risk she took.'

She sighed against him. 'You can't tell me you haven't noticed it.'

'Noticed what?'

She sounded cross. 'That she's kissed the earth you've walked on since you were six. She wouldn't think of the risk.'

He didn't grasp what she meant because she was bustling him along too much. 'Oh, Mum, and then for the gun not to go off.'

He surprised her with that remark. 'You've got to load them first. Thank God she didn't think of it and now won't get the chance. Pan Pacific have the gun!'

'But what if they punish her?' he said. 'Mum, you've got to let me go back.'

Her hand was tighter, propelling him. 'It's not our job to get mixed up any more with that. Your brothers are locked in the house. They're only babies. We've got to look after them until the men come home.'

'Mum, I can't walk out on Leah.'

He tried to break free of her, but she was determined to hold him captive. 'Gratitude's one thing,' she said, 'stupidity is another. You're going to cool down and get cleaned up. You are *not* going back. Leah will not be touched. She's off the street. Even Pan Pacific wouldn't force an entry on the shop.' It was surprising how strong she was, a woman who was always crying weak. He was propelled by her sideways through a gap in the convoy, across the street, and through his own gate, taking with him in the eye of his mind an impression of Leah crumbling as men disarmed her by force. Leah Elliot, Leah the mouse. (Who'd kissed the ground he had walked on since he was six?) And an impression of himself thrown like baggage to the wall of the shop; Shane Baxter huddled in a heap while a girl fought and women shrieked down the street.

'See,' his mother said, 'we're home, we're safe. If you ignore them they let you pass, as of course they must.'

He had not expected her to say that. There was a meaning to it he did not like. 'We *have* run out!'

'Put any construction on it you like. I'm a woman and you're still a child. Handling that is man's work.'

'We *have* run out! You don't know at all that Leah's all right.'

She had the key in the door and the fingers of her other hand pinched so tightly into his upper arm that the pain was like an injection stabbed bluntly in the wrong place. 'Shane, please,' she said, and thrust him inside, 'there'll be no argument. I know what I'm doing and I'm doing right. If they'd listened to me an hour ago we'd be in nothing like this mess.' Two small boys were under her feet. 'Yes, Gary; yes, Brendan; you can see that I'm back. Now run yourself a bath, Shane, and I'll fix some dinner, if I can scrape it off the dish. Remember, if anyone goes out it'll be a hiding when your father gets back. You're to stay in the house.'

Shane groped miserably to his room, rubbing his arm, with a four-year-old and a seven-year-old tracking at his heels, as they might have done any other day of the week. How could things as ordinary as kid brothers still exist?

'Shane, do you hear that?'

'Hear what?'

'About going out.'

'Yes, Mum, I heard.'

'Now run your bath.' She was calling from the kitchen, clattering crockery.

'Yes, Mum, I'll run it; give us a chance. I've got to get some clothes, haven't I? I can't walk round stark.'

'Jeans. Blue-checked shirt. I'll bring them to the bathroom.'

'Strike me, Mum. Don't you know what I've been through? Crikey, Gary, I know it's your room, too, but I wish you'd stop chattering or get lost.'

He leant against the window, with his nose to the glass, not really looking out, feeling like a failure in everything he had ever done or felt. Blooming Auntie Sadie. Imagine it, not showing her face. Imagine *her* chickening out.

Auntie Sadie's house stuck on that hillock like a wart on a witch's nose. Auntie Sadie on her broomstick never splendidly in flight, not for a little boy of years ago expectant at night, nor for a lad of nearly fifteen whose heart wanted to break. Auntie Sadie's hillock would be part of the hole along with everything else. Normie and Cherry in shimmering heat scrambling for the ridge behind the chimney pots, Normie with his gun, Cherry looking unladylike (typical) with dress blowing up.

'Crumbs,' Shane groaned, 'no one's got a hope.'

Two men were striding from step to step up the path from Aunt Sadie's gate. Another was scaling the lattice between the corner verandah posts. Knowing what they were about. Eliminating the kids. Stamping on the crazy ones like they were ants. Tidying up the place for a nice clean start.

So a fellow went along with his girl's bright ideas and got himself caught on a roof. Normie could have shrieked.

'No,' he'd said, 'no, you drip. It's too soon. You've just gotta wait. It's not like before when they were looking at Shane and Leah, now they're looking for *us*.'

But she stuck her head out round the side of the chimney, sticky-beaking, and wham, got caught so fast it was as quick as a shot. Got nailed fair and square across a hot tin roof, hot enough to fry eggs, hot enough to bake a cake. Down by the chimney they'd sat on a sack, but you couldn't cart a sack up a slope like the face of a cliff, not with a gun in one hand and a girl snatching for you so often it was a wonder your pants stayed up. Of course a fellow should never have gone for the ridge. He should have gone down over the edge, clunk, and headed helter-skelter for the bush. But you couldn't think of everything in a flash, and tumbling down a grape-vine in a few seconds flat was a different kettle of fish from taking it nice and easy going up. Yeh, he could have shrieked, because it was the craziest sort of roof, like a volcano with one high point, and a twelve-foot drop to flagstone paths that he didn't want to think about. So on impulse he had headed for the top. A fellow had to run somewhere. Where else but to the top, where he could sit like Joey and hold them off? Where worse with a dead-weight girl slipping and slithering behind you like she was about to vanish into space?

'Let go my leg. Do you want us dead? Lemme get up first.'

But she cried back like someone drowning in mud. 'I can't let go.'

'Of course you can.'

'I'll fall, Normie.'

'By crikey, you'd better not.'

'I'm scared, Normie.'

'Well whose fault's that? Who stuck out her silly-looking head?'

They were sprawled over the iron, about five stupid feet from the top, like a couple of sizzling steaks.

'For crying out loud, Cherry, I'm fryin' in me own fat. If you don't let go I reckon I'll lash out.'

'Normie, you wouldn't do that.'

He wouldn't either, but he was getting desperate. Climbing roofs was kids' stuff, but not with her hanging on the back. 'Dig in your fingernails or something. Stick on with spit. But lemme get to the top. I won't leave you there. I'll pull you up. Fair dinkum, Cherry, we'll cook. Stupid roof it is. Why's it so steep?'

But her clutching fingers had gone. He was surprised and looked giddily down. Her face pale with fear, screaming without sound, was sliding away in jerks, stopping and starting. Eye to eye in despair, they slid apart, then one stop lasted longer. It lasted for excruciating seconds and lasted longer still. Oh,

Cherry, Cherry, Cherry. You're not a body's length from the edge. You could have been dead. Cherry with hands clawed pressed to the iron, and feet splayed, still looking up eye to eye, saying '*Normie, help.*'

He was hoarse and almost sick, his sense of balance was unsure and his own security was hit or miss. 'Spit again, Cherry. . . . There wasn't enough stick . . .'

Her eyes closed and shut him out and there was nothing to read on her face.

It was the end of it. How could he go up? How could he go down? Shouting at Cherry and calling her for everything in the book; he had not meant a word of it. Firing off guns and climbing on roofs; how stupid could you get? Stupid, stupid, stupid. Climbing a roof for what? For playing big heroes. For showing off.

She was looking at him again and her eyes were bloodshot and heat was burning through the fabric of his clothes almost to the flesh. What was it doing to her whose clothes were so much less?

'Cherry, go back to the chimney.'

She shook her head.

'It's probably not as hard as it looks. Slip back a little bit. Get your toes in the guttering and edge along.'

She shook her head.

There was another face. Beyond Cherry, diagonally past the chimney at about thirty feet, a man rolled over the gutter line above the corner verandah posts, rolled on to the roof, stretched flat, and looked up. Which man was it? Which face from the crowd was it? Which particular hammer would he be using to break up Chinaman's Reef?

Cherry panted, 'Is someone there?'

'Yeh, a bloke.'

'Will he help?'

Slowly the man settled himself, turned on to his back, edged his legs over the side, gripped the guttering like grim death, then suddenly sat up. It was a miracle he didn't fall off. Cautiously, he placed his hands in his lap and began to look comfortable, even safe, but the glance he gave the ground might have implied something else.

Someone out of sight called from below, 'Are you O.K., mate?'

'The iron's flamin' hot.' But the eye he had on Normie was made of stern stuff. 'Let the rifle go, boy. Unload it and slide it down the roof. Give it a push and it won't stop for breath.'

'My girl needs help.'

'If she's your girl, boy, get rid of the rifle quick. You can't give her better help than that.'

'I'm not talking about rifles.'

'But I am. That rifle's bigger trouble than anything else you've got.'

'*She might slip off.*'

'And who will you blame for that?'

Cherry wasn't saying a word. She was clinging there with her eyes shut and Normie sensed her mother and his own mother emerging arm in arm out of the mass of vehicles cramming the street. It was a vague awareness, almost like a fleeting thought. Then he pitted his nerve against his uncertain balance and deliberately raised himself from the roof to squat sideways, one leg extended as a brace.

'Cherry,' he said, 'see what I've done. It's easy. Fair dinkum it is.'

She wouldn't look.

'Please, Cherry.'

'I can't, I can't. Oh, Normie, I think I'm burning up.'

'The rifle, boy. We don't lift a finger until you play your part.'

'That's blackmail, Mister.'

'Is it? How do you figure that one out?'

Blooming man sitting there safe, sitting there smug, and Normie remembered which face from the crowd it was. That fellow had manhandled him, had snatched him up from the road on the far side of town and tossed him in the scrub. O.K., Mister, get tossed yourself!

Normie's nerves were jumping right down to his feet but he swung the rifle up to his shoulder, good and straight, and that fellow was over the edge with a mighty leap and must have hit the path like a ton of bricks. 'Don't you put a price on my girl,' Normie shrieked and recklessly crabbed down to her, skidding only once, and braced himself beside her as he had done higher up. There was shouting below, with references to himself, but

Normie ignored it. 'I'm the anchor, Cherry. Pull yourself up.'
There was something extra special about the way her hands
used him, a warm and wonderful feeling of dependence and
trust, that helped him to stay there, that actually made him
stick. Then her arm went tightly round his waist and she was
alongside him, for the moment safe. 'Cherry Cooper; I'd have
died if you'd fallen off.' But he was too shy to say anything as
sloppy as that.

'Normie.'

'Yeh.'

'We can't stay here. My clothes are too thin. I feel as though
half my skin's burnt off.'

'It's not.'

'Oh, Normie, I've got you in a proper fix.'

He shrugged. 'Have you? What have I done wrong? Tell me
what? Except for shooting off a gun on Sunday. I even aimed
at me own house and I'll bet the bullet mark is on the chimney
to prove it.' He disengaged his arm and pulled off his shirt.
'Here,' he said, 'stick it under your legs; it'll break the heat.'
Then he knotted the corners of his handkerchief and made a
cap of it for her head. 'We're stopping here,' he said, sounding
full of confidence, 'let *them* do the worrying.' But he was
cracking hardy and Cherry knew it. She was thinking of things
like sunstroke. So was Normie. Of things like sunstroke and the
gun and of prison doors clanging shut and of not knowing what
to do except sit. It had been a storm in a teacup. The storm had
blown out.

Their mothers were on the road a yard or two from Auntie
Sadie's gate, limply arm in arm, looking up. Something about
the way they stood seemed to say that they had had enough.
They looked like visitors to a strange place, made dull by un-
accustomed pressures, overawed by belligerent crowds and
jostling streets. They had nothing to say to each other or even
to Pan Pacific. Men calling on them from Auntie Sadie's garden
were ignored. Others passing with a ladder unstrapped from a
truck were compelled to manoeuvre around them because, with
bovine emptiness, they would not budge from the approach to
the gate. They said nothing to Normie or Cherry either. Just
looked up, as Normie and Cherry just sat.

Shane, leaning on the window with his nose pressed to the glass, seeing it all, with two little kids clamouring round his feet, Mum clattering things in the kitchen with stubborn indifference though the view from her window was the same as his. 'I know what I'm doing,' Mum had said, 'and I'm doing right. If they'd listened to me an hour ago they'd be in nothing like this mess.' What had Mum said an hour ago? Nothing of note that Shane could remember unless she'd said it when he wasn't about. Chinaman's was dying meekly on its back.

A ladder swung from the ground like a pendulum upside down and struck the side of Auntie Sadie's house, Shane feeling it as if it had struck himself, Normie and Cherry looking at it, passively, sitting like nervous spectators on a grandstand roof. Pan Pacific gathering round, stumbling over Auntie Sadie's garden as if plants were nothing and flowers were dirt. You'd have thought Auntie Sadie would have come out to poke them with her broomstick or to order them off the place. But Auntie Sadie wasn't the type. Everyone knew they owned her house. Everyone knew she had been given its use, free of rent, for the duration of her life. Grandpa Baxter used to chuckle his head off. 'They reckoned she'd die young, poor frail thing. They thought they'd be rid of her in a year or two. They never reckoned on her living until they were all dead themselves. Sadie Stevenson laughs last.'

But she wasn't laughing last. They were driving her out—or maybe they'd dig the hole with the hillock left in the middle, sheer cliffs all around, and her garden gate opening on a hundred-foot drop. Why didn't she fight? Imagine it; not showing her face.

'Shane! That *bath*!'

'Yeh, Mum.'

Now a fellow was shinning up the ladder and Normie and Cherry were sitting together close like a couple of birds waiting to be picked off by hawks.

It sort of hurt.

'Shane!'

'Yeh, Mum, I'm on my way.'

But suddenly his spirit revolted and he heaved on his window sash with a deliberate jerk and shot it to the top with a crash.

He then leapt or tripped or fell, bearing the insect screen before him to the hard earth, smashing it in splinters of powdering wood and rusted fragments of mesh. He sprawled in it, prickling and sneezing from its metallic dust, but if holding Chinaman's together was man's work, the nearest thing to a man was himself. His brothers were squealing somewhere like infants in a fright, his mother was thudding on the kitchen window glass, her face a twisted mask of itself.

He picked himself up and ran and vaulted the fence into the street, but the leap from inside to outside lasted through an age of doubt. He found himself standing foolishly on the footpath with no conception of what he should do next, confronted by a wall of metal and huge rubber tyres and caterpillar tracks dormant on low loaders and grown men and hopelessness.

His face lengthened, his mouth drooped, and his mother was breathing heavily at his side. 'Shane, darling,' she said, and put an arm round his shoulders, 'I understand. I know. But there's nothing we can do; is there? We're hurting only ourselves. They're much bigger than us.'

A man was standing on Auntie Sadie's roof using the projecting top of the ladder to support himself. He extended an arm like a policeman on point duty. 'This way,' that arm said, 'I own the earth.'

'Mum, why didn't Auntie Sadie come out?'

'I don't know, darling. It almost seems she's not at home.'

Cherry was coming down the ladder and Shane shivered, because no one was prouder than Cherry. Proud and wild. Cherry climbing meekly down the ladder like a little girl caught doing wrong. Cherry Cooper was nothing to Pan Pacific.

'Mum, we had to *try*. We couldn't let them walk over us.'

'All right, then; you tried.'

Normie was coming down the ladder without his gun.

'Mum, we haven't got anywhere to live.'

'No, darling. That's true.'

'But Chinaman's belongs to us.'

'It doesn't and it never has. We lived here on borrowed time. We thought it would never happen. But everything in this world happens sooner or later.'

She sounded very knowing and very sad and somehow

Shane's younger brothers had come to occupy the mantle of her other arm. They weren't even chattering; they were simply there, clinging round her skirts.

'Mum, don't give up.'

'It has nothing to do with giving up. They're in the right. Some things you must accept.'

'They *can't* be right. Chinaman's belongs to us.'

'Darling, I'm not even sure that I wish it did.'

Normie and Cherry being shepherded down to Auntie Sadie's gate like undesirables being shown the way out. Shane couldn't hear a word but could guess what was being said. 'It's my gun; I want it back.' 'You must be joking, kid. Send us your new address and we'll forward it on.' 'What do you mean, my new address?' 'Wherever you bed down, kid, Timbuktu or wherever else.'

Cherry and Normie, hand in hand, facing their mothers. Standing there as if they had just been introduced and would rather not have met.

'It's not the end for you, darling,' Shane's mother said, 'it's the beginning of something better. Instead of going away on your own in a year or two, we'll go now, all of us, together. Chinaman's isn't much of a place. You can't even choose your friends; there isn't any choice. It's a tiny, tiny world. It's dead. All it's fit for is an open cut.'

He looked at her, shocked, and she was staring straight ahead, seeing nothing, crying huge tears.

'Mum, you don't mean it, do you? You don't mean what you say?'

'I do mean it,' she said, 'I do mean what I say.'

'You sound like that horrible man Gibbs.'

'Really. That "horrible man", as you call him, must be wiser than you think. Shane, I cannot continue this conversation. You must come indoors.'

It was true. Chinaman's had fallen apart from within. One little push and all the King's horses and all the King's men couldn't put it together again.

Normie's mother suddenly broke her silence. 'If you stand there much longer with that stupid look I think I'll slap your face.'

Normie shrugged.

'My mind boggles, Normie Muir, that a boy of thirteen could start all this.'

'Start what?' cried Cherry. 'You went rushing off to throw your rock and he didn't even have the gun. If you've got to blame Normie, you've got to blame me and yourself and everybody else. You've got to blame the crummy Pan Pacific and the fathers for running off and Auntie Sadie for sneaking out the back. She could have stopped it any time she liked.'

'Cherry, Cherry,' her mother sighed, 'hold your tongue. You're not talking sense. Let us save what little dignity we have left.'

CHAPTER TEN

Lord High Executioner

PETER COOPER, aged six, sat on a hard-backed chair, legs crossed, arms folded, feet marooned in space. 'There's trouble outside,' his mother had said, ages and ages ago, 'so stay there, Peter, don't you move or speak a word to anyone until I get back.' Peter—as almost always—was faithful to his trust. 'You keep an eye on Mr Gibbs and don't get off your chair.' She had grabbed the poker from the open fireplace, weighed it for a moment in her hand, but dropped it with a clatter back on the bricks. Then she had run.

Peter had fixed his eyes with gravity on the man on the couch. He had cushions under his head and blood on his shirt and perspiration on his face and a bandage over his forehead and a huge wrist watch and restless hands that he wiped often on his handkerchief. (The handkerchief was *very* dirty; even worse than his own with chewing-gum on it.) They stared silently at each other until the man looked somewhere else, perhaps at the ceiling of ornately pressed tin, or the family photographs on the mantelshelf, or the television set, or Cherry's piano, or the armchairs, or the round table with heavy legs all somehow arranged together in that small and airless place. Then his eyes would come back to Peter's stare, to be held until the strain again began to hurt in ways that had nothing to do with the wound in his head.

Two other men came blundering back in, they had left not long before, and these also Peter regarded with scarcely a blink, huge eyes like lamps of low lustre, watched them into the room with such intensity that their voices dropped to undertones and one of them tripped on the mat.

'Blast,' the man said, and Peter frowned so severely that the man took out a handkerchief (also very dirty) and mopped his

122

neck and bald head. Auntie Stevenson didn't like words like that. 'Flamin' kids,' he said, 'kids, kids, kids.' Then they started whispering and Peter's ears cocked up. He didn't really know who said what or what they meant—but Peter always listened to his elders with rapt attention—and every time a word was bad he clicked his tongue with disapproval and one man or the other would shift his feet or scratch his head or mop his neck. 'That kid,' one of them grumbled, 'must know every word in the book.' But Peter kept his eyes on Mr Gibbs, sometimes swaying widely to the left, sometimes to the right, to see round the men. His stare was like a beam of light, destroying privacy, from which the man on the couch could not escape. But Peter didn't know that and would not have understood. Peter listened and stared and did as his mother had said.

'Is he Lord High Executioner or what?'

'He lives here, Kennedy,' the man on the couch said. 'He can be no more than five or six.'

'He makes me nervous, Mr Gibbs.'

'Yes, he makes me nervous as well.'

Remarks which interested Peter because he felt sure they were about himself. Other matters were less direct, like listening to television through the bedroom wall when the lights were out, fitting pictures to words that jumped all over the place.

'You wouldn't thank us, sir, if we dragged it off. You can't wreck a ten-thousand-dollar motor car. If we lift it off nice and easy we'll not even scratch the paint, but it's not a simple matter like jacking it up. You've run on to a stump and stuck her good and hard until we can bring a crane through to the front. We've had half a dozen men on her; can't budge her an inch. You've got that caravan bearing down behind it on the camber into the ditch; if we uncouple it we'll be in all the trouble about the place. And how do we get a crane through, tell me that? We've got a mess, Mr Gibbs.'

'You haven't seen outside, sir. You can't move out there. We're all piled up one on top of the other. It's a ridiculous street. We're too long and too wide for it, but no one's laughing at the joke.'

Peter smiled, however, because they did *say* it was a joke.

'We can't turn round, we can't go ahead, and we can't reverse. The idiots that have tried have only made it worse.'

'I'm not to believe that you can't reverse?'

'We can't, Mr Gibbs. Johnston and Turner are rammed back there. Front to back. They can't even prise them apart. When you stopped, you stopped. You must have speeded up to twenty-five—and you stopped!'

'We've got machines here, as you know, Mr Gibbs, that'll shift anything about the place. But there's not much you can do when you can't get them off the loaders.'

'Look, anywhere else we'd have time to sit down and nut it out, or wait for extra equipment to come in, but in this crazy dump we're sitting ducks. We don't know from minute to minute what's going to happen next.'

'They're mad, Mr Gibbs. Half a dozen women and kids. Stark, staring mad.'

'Shotguns and rifles. Telephones smashed. We can't even ring the police.'

'They come leaping out of doors and windows.'

'Screaming like banshees.'

'Racing over rooftops.'

'It's a madhouse.'

'Johnston got bitten!'

'His arm, so help me. A kid's teeth. Crunch.'

Peter's eyes turned into huge round question-marks.

'We know you've had a knock, Mr Gibbs, and mightn't be feeling like thinking things out, but we've got to have your authority to protect ourselves.'

The man on the couch almost raised himself up, but had to sink back. 'No, Kennedy. Enough's enough.'

'We see it this way, Mr Gibbs. Why not start up a dozer, turn it on its tracks, and drive it over the side of the loader? The worst we can do is damage the loader a bit.'

'What use is that?'

'Bring it along the footpath. Knock over a few trees and verandah posts. Flatten a house or a shop and bust out through the side. Cut ourselves a road of our own, no less.'

'The men are edgy, sir. We want some action. We didn't come here to be done to death by kids.'

'I don't see the point! To me everything seems to be quiet.'

'Look, sir, we don't like being caged up like this. If you try to play it calm, it blows up in your face. We say send a dozer out through the side and they'll know what they're up against. A dozer on the rampage is a sobering sight, and showing a strong arm might be saving a life. You know me, Mr Gibbs, I don't scare, but we've got trouble. Two guns already. How many more have they got hidden about the place?'

'Kennedy's right, Mr Gibbs; we all back him to the hilt. If we don't take a stand someone's going to get hurt—'

'And I'm not hurt?'

'You prove our point, sir. Cut that road through in the right place and we can clear the street. There might be easier ways of doing it but this way they learn who's boss.'

'We've been scouting round, Mr Gibbs. There's an old road out the back. Break through to it and we've got a straight run to the railway yards. Then camp there and we can see all directions at once. We're outside, on the spot, and you're not.'

'There's a law in the land. I think you're losing sight of it.'

'With all due respect, sir; does Pan Pacific own the town or does it not?'

Gibbs sighed. 'Every square foot.'

'Well then, if we can knock over thirty buildings next week, we can flatten one today. It's self-defence . . .'

They left, glancing quickly at Peter as they went, Peter still staring, still sitting on his chair, arms folded and legs crossed, and it was too much for the man on the couch. He started groaning within himself and had to force his feet to the floor and nurse his head in his hands, simply to escape.

A pain, both dull and sharp, seemed centred at the nape of his neck and the rest of his head felt as big as a house. He knew what had happened in a vague sort of way but had no clear memory of separate events. The blow on the head seemed to have split him into quantities of anger and remorse and spite, into parts out of balance, inexplicably changing their importance. The assault on his person was an outrage, of course. It was also something else, because there were qualities in these people that no reasonable man could have expected in advance.

They had stood up to something ten thousand times larger than themselves and fought.

They bewildered him. He had come on a Sunday specifically to minimize risk, but it had gone the wrong way, totally, and then they had fought. And then had set a boy on him; a large-eyed child with an extraordinary power to hurt. Fifty years ago he had been the same age himself, living across the street.

'Mr Gibbs, you must lie down. I insist.'

It was the woman again, the one who had dressed his head, mother of the child whose eyes he no longer wished to face.

'I'm sitting up, madam, because if I don't I'll be sick.'

'You will do as I tell you,' she said, 'or leave my house.'

He smiled wanly, very faintly, and put down his head, recognizing in the woman a professional trademark. 'You were a nurse?'

'Yes.'

'There's not to be a doctor?'

'I can't say and couldn't care. But you were not hit by a cannon shell. You *swooned*, Mr Gibbs, from fright, and suffered a gash and bled like a pig, which all seems fair enough.'

'Madam,' he said thinly, 'it isn't fair enough; it's most unjust.'

But she walked out, a road-mender's wife, humiliating him by her perfect sense of timing, by knowing exactly what to say and when to stop, but left her huge-eyed child behind her, or forgot him, sitting on his chair mutely keeping watch. 'Lord,' the man said, and turned away his head, resenting the boy and his tired-looking mother in her cheap-looking dress and her proud dominion over her tenth-rate house—and bewildered by doubt. He would have followed her if he had had the strength, not to demand an apology, but to defend and justify himself. Then he would have struggled on to the street, calling after Kennedy. Kennedy was a good employee, but he had a vindictive streak. 'No, it's too great a risk. Haven't we already proved that it's not the way to stop people from getting hurt? What could you have said that made me agree to it?' But the room was quiet and hot and almost airless, smelling of age, somehow remote from the street. Nothing could disturb it, nothing could happen; not while that monstrous child sat there like a god of fate.

'Hullo, Cherry,' the boy said.

The man, with a start, looked up. The doorway was shadowed by a striking girl in white who caught the glow from the open front door of the house.

The girl who had flung herself at his car and almost stopped his heart with fright had also been dressed in white; that girl who had driven him on to the impact of a rock in the face. Was white symbolic? Were they bent on shaming him to death?

She had a young woman's radiance, but was only a child grown up too fast. Her dress was soiled, her hair was all over the place, a scratch scored her right arm from the elbow to the wrist, and she stared with insolence. Her eyes were as sombre as those of the boy, but held extra meaning. He could feel her frigid judgment bearing against him and he could not front up to it. In a completely different way it hurt, because this young girl was aware of herself and of the things that men thought. Her insolence told him that, and her scorn let him know that he was beneath her contempt.

That he cared in the least for the scorn of a child bewildered him. He could not understand himself. He wanted to sit up and shout: 'Why? Why? Why judge me? Why hit me on the head with a rock? Why hate me like dirt? What have I done that anyone couldn't see coming a mile off? It's not God's holy acre. It's a dump. Tin-pot, tumbledown town. A wreck. Why turn me into an ogre? I'm doing nothing that in my place you wouldn't do yourselves. Why make me feel that I'm stealing bread off your plates? Listen, girl, it was obvious fifty years ago that the only way to work the field without risking life was an open cut. So you've had fifty years' grace. What more do you want? Pan Pacific's not a gang of crooks. We *own* the place, bought and paid for it in 1888. There's never been any question of digging it up by permission or favour of anyone else. It's ours, and what you've had you've leased from us at bedrock rents. Ask your parents. Ask your grandparents. Ask the history books.' But he said nothing because he knew that to her even the truth would have sounded false. A fast-revving engine fired somewhere close and added to his agonies of indecision. Did the girl know, as he knew, that it was an auxiliary unit that would swing a bulldozer engine into life? If she knew she batted not an eyelid nor an inch.

'Don't you know I'm doing you a favour? Don't you know you're getting second-best?' But again he asked her only within himself, not using his voice. 'Don't you know the outside world is a wonderful place? What's going to happen to you here? They'll marry you off to some local lout. You'll be bearing babies before you know what life's about. That silly old woman playing God at the end of the street is a curse on girls like you. How many have grown up here because of her when you could have grown up in a civilized place? What's your mother but half the person she could be anywhere else? What's to become of *him* over there, that monster on the chair?

'I was born here, too; what do you think of that? But I'm one of the lucky ones and can't remember her face. They took me away when I was six.

'Insane conceit of the woman, accepting her father's guilt. What guilt was there, except the sentimental stupidity of shooting himself? You can't blame a man for a fault in the earth. If it were not for her outrageous conceit, Chinaman's Reef would be decently extinct and your father would have a decent job and your mother a decent house and you would be princess of a civilized street.'

But not a word of it came out, and only when her eyes shifted, with a cool and deliberate drop, did he realize what he had done. He had opened his hand towards her, appealing for Heaven knows what, and instantly she stepped from his sight, cutting him dead. So he said to the boy, sitting on his chair, 'I came in here today feeling pretty good. What's gone wrong? I knew where I was going and what I was about.'

But the fast-revving engine on the street merged in a sound of far greater volume, shaking the house and unseating Peter, who rushed to the window to look out. The holland blind crashed up and the glare flooded in like a force that made the man flinch. He felt suddenly exposed, suddenly guilty of an infamous act. He was himself the god of fate and the Lord High Executioner. Words like those had nothing to do with the harmless little boy in the light.

CHAPTER ELEVEN

Interval Taken Out of Time

LEAH heard the big engine roar and looked directly at her mother, not any more in the way of an obedient child. The woman saw in her daughter's eyes something that other parents spoke about but that she had not seen in her house before. Leah's manner projected impatience and hostility in the manner of a person with strength of her own who didn't want to be bothered with other people's views.

'That's a bulldozer,' Leah said, raising her voice, turning a simple statement into a declaration of independence.

She had heard bulldozers before, and she knew now which one it was; that huge machine on that huge low-loader not fifty feet from the shop verandah.

Mrs Elliot deliberately turned to her half-cold, half-eaten meal, even though food repulsed her and to ignore the bulldozer and what it meant to herself and to Leah was absurd. Even though the vibration of its sound made her want to run and hide.

'That's a bulldozer, Mum,' Leah shouted, and pushed her chair from the table. 'We can't let them do as they please. It's our town! Who do they think they are?'

Suddenly the woman went for her and grabbed at Leah's back, clutching a handful of her dress. 'You're not going outside, Leah, you're not, you're not. It's over. It's finished with. I forbid it absolutely.'

But Leah dragged her mother after her towards the door that opened on to the lane.

'No, no, *no*,' the woman shouted, 'didn't they shame you enough before?' With a desperate spasm she ripped the dress apart down the seam and fell with a strip of cloth in her hand. Then she sat on the floor and inexplicably cried. Leah looked down, 'Oh, Mum . . . Did you have to do that? Why that?'

'You're not going, Leah. I forbid it absolutely. You're not moving from here until they've gone.'

It was odd how illogical grown-ups could be.

Shane heard the big engine roar and sat up in his bath. 'Mum,' he yelled. 'What's that?'

It was like a prison not being able to see out. The only window, above his head, was a fixed louvre of three narrow blades of opaque glass facing away from the street.

'Mum, that's a bulldozer. . . . Gary, where's my towel? You haven't brought me a towel. Mum, my clothes. Where are my clothes?' He stood up, stranded in the bath. 'Mum, what'd they start a bulldozer for? They couldn't be thinking of pushing us over *now*?'

No one answered.

'Hey, Mum. There are no towels. I can't dry myself.'

Perhaps someone came to the door; it was hard to be sure; then walked away.

'Hey. You could have chucked the towel in. There's no bath-mat here. I'll have to puddle across the floor.'

But no one came back and Shane yelled, 'Can't you hear me or what?'

Perhaps there was too much noise.

So he puddled to the door and found his answers. There was a stout gate hook outside, high on the door, put there to keep generations of toddlers out of the bathroom during the day. It hadn't been used for a year or two. 'Hey,' Shane yelled, outraged. 'What'd you lock it for? Let me out of here!'

But no one replied.

'So you give up,' he yelled, 'but they keep on going, don't they? They start up bulldozers. They fight real brave when no one fights back. You know what they're doing, don't you? They're kicking you when you're down. Let me out of here.'

He sat heavily on the edge of the bath and clenched his teeth. 'How do you like that? If they can't stop a fella by fair means they stop him by foul. They stick him in a bath. They take away his clothes. They lock the door.'

'Hey,' he screeched, 'I'm not five; I'm nearly fifteen. You can't treat me this way.'

But no one came.

Mrs Albert Muir stood with her back to the wall, arms folded, two keys in her clenched right hand, the key to the front door and the key to the back door. If there had been keys to the windows she would have held them as well. She looked enormous and was flushed to a faintly purple hue. Mum and the bulldozer were of the same breed, both built about as big as they could be.

'No, Normie, you've had my final say. I don't care what it is, I don't care what it means, I just don't care.'

'Look, Mum—'

'You can argue, Normie, until you're black in the face. The answer's *no*.'

He felt frantic, like a creature on the run caught in a snare. 'Look, Maureen, you tell her. Clara, you tell her. Tell her someone's got to stand up to them. So we made a muck of it before; that doesn't mean it'll happen again.'

'You're dead right, my boy, it *won't*. Your father will kill me when he gets home. "Let's do it peaceful," he said. "If there's one thing I've learnt in my life," he said, "that this morning's proved again, it's don't get tough with your betters. If you belong to a trade union," he said, "with twenty thousand mates, you can take on the world. If you live in Chinaman's Reef you don't rate a poke in the eye".'

You couldn't get through; it was like beating your head against a wall. 'But, Mum, I wouldn't do anything silly. You know me.'

'Between the two of us, young man, aren't we in enough trouble for one day?' Then she shut her mouth, tightly, deliberately, and sat herself at the kitchen table and proceeded to butter a slice of bread. 'Maureen,' she said, 'sit down. Clara, you too. Normie, sit!'

'But, Mum—'

'*Sit!*'

Normie sat. The knife beside his plate was shivering from the vibration of the bulldozer engine transmitted through the earth. The salt-shaker was shivering. The egg-timer on the wall was swinging to and fro. Normie snarled, 'It's monkey business they're up to, for sure. What do they want a bulldozer for?'

'Be quiet, Normie.'

'They've only got to unhook Gibbs's caravan and push it off the road and then they can get through. As big as it is, you can't tell me forty or fifty blokes can't manhandle *that* out of the way.'

'Normeee . . .' His mother raised a threatening hand.

'It's only the caravan that's blocking the road. Nothin' else. Holy cow, I was up on Auntie Sadie's roof watching them for half the time. I'm tellin' you, they didn't *try*. All they were doing was talking and waving their arms around. I'm tellin' you, they're goin' to run that dozer through us just to be good and nasty.'

Mrs Muir's hand swept across the table and struck Normie on the shoulder with an impact that jarred him to the bone. Cups and saucers and sugar basin crashed to the floor, the salt-shaker broke against the wall. Normie's lips quivered, but it was Clara who cried.

'This is my house,' Mrs Muir said. 'What I say, goes.'

It was awful. It was cruel. That bulldozer was making a horrible row. It was off the loader, surely, and on the ground. It was thudding like a battering ram and there were horrible cracks like trees coming down. Normie clenched his fists and set his jaw and ordered himself not to cry. Strike a fellow dead; what *were* they doing outside? Oddly and suddenly, all he longed for was Cherry by the hand and a walk of miles and miles, but it wasn't Cherry that he found; his mother's pink and fleshy hand reached across the table and gave his wrist a squeeze. 'Try to see it, Normie,' she said, 'there's nothing we can do.' Mum was blubbing of course, so was Clara, and now Maureen. He sighed and every bruise and scratch he had collected that day started hurting like mad, even the patched-up cut on his backside. He had to sniff, but flatly refused to cry; someone in the house had to be the man; even when the bulldozer seemed to be at the very door.

As it was.

Operated by the man called Kennedy, it crabbed along the footpath in a deliberately irregular line, dislodging and fragmenting paving stones, screwing them under its tracks as a man might extinguish with his shoe a spent cigarette, scoring the trunks of peppercorn-trees and tearing down boughs even where they did not obstruct the way, uprooting fence-posts and age-old hitching posts with the edges of its blade, crushing growing things that had lived for sixty and seventy and eighty years.

Cherry drooped at her mother's bedroom window, looking out on a shuddering world where not a man moved on foot, where there was not a human face except behind windscreen glass. There they presided, dimly seen, not like living men, but like figures of wax that might eerily stir on command. Cherry leant there and cried a little and felt a million years alone. Vehicles obstructed her view but allowed anguished glimpses of a yellow-painted monster nervily squirting black puffs of smoke and thrusting itself about in jerks and stabs in an ill-tempered way, each thrust bearing behind it thirty tons of steel. Trees tossing over there on Normie's side of the street as if a gale blew, dust rising up, splitting sounds, a screaming tabby cat startlingly stark, like the flying head of a broom shooting from somewhere on the road over Cherry's face as if bent on penetrating her window pane, but alighting in the garden and vanishing down the side, scarcely touching the ground.

Still startling her moments after it had gone. Still flying over the fence, again and again in her mind although it had gone, startling all the words away that she wanted to shout at that mechanical horror outside.

That bulldozer, now anxious for another game, turned ninety degrees and Cherry knew exactly what it would do, although no one had told her and the machine itself she could not perfectly see. A fence was there, adjoining Normie's house, and she knew it was crushed to the ground. A garden was there, parts of it long dead, parts long overgrown, and she knew the blade tore it all through. A house was there, the Lindsay house, empty for years, and she saw it collapse like a mound of sand undermined, a weird subsidence that became a dust cloud, termite dust and earth dust and spider dust and brick dust and the dust of rusty iron, a horrible, billowing mess of dust and a horrible rending sound like a cry.

Oh, it was every house in town crying from the pain. It was

the cry of every house dying in its own turn. Cherry's house, too. Every house a dust cloud, a dirt cloud, rubbish and ruin. How could it be true? How could it happen with not a man or a woman or a boy or a girl to be seen?

Something exploded inside her and suddenly she was no longer at her mother's window but in the other front room punching at the man on the couch, hitting him again and again, even hitting at the arm he threw up to shield his head until her own arms were trapped and pinned to her sides by a bear hug from behind. She fought the hug, for the moment not understanding it, but could not dislodge it. She fought it until fighting it exhausted her and she was guided to a deep chair and forced into it. Then her mother sat on the arm beside her bearing heavily on her shoulder. 'Cherry, Cherry,' she sighed, 'some things are inexcusable.' Cherry heard, even though the house still shook and noises unlike notes touched by hands came from the piano.

'Meaning him,' she said, 'or me?' But said it so weakly that it was scarcely more than a thought lost in the noise. The pressure of her mother's hand changed character, no longer bearing down, but comforting her, and Peter came from the window and sat on the other arm of the chair, and everything became less horrible than it had seemed. In a curious sort of way it became a family portrait, all three sitting there, an old-fashioned portrait taken in the days when Chinaman's first became a town and you sat still, you obediently froze, you didn't breathe or blink or twitch, and the man with the camera bulb in his hand counted the seconds away. And afterwards things never seemed to be quite the same; an interval had been taken out of time and preserved for a very special purpose, for looking at afterwards, for remembering, for pasting in a frame, for taking with you when you grew up and left home.

The man on the couch struggled to a sitting position and eased his feet to the floor. He knew he had to go. The family wasn't his; his face did not belong there; but it was an awful effort raising himself until he could stand. He tried to apologize with a bow then shuffled from the room and left the house by the front door. But he couldn't stop it now that it had started. What did it matter when or how Chinaman's Reef was pushed down? Next week or today? It was the same. After all, he too was only a cog in the machine, and the house that Kennedy had chosen to eliminate for his temporary road might easily have been the house where Malcolm Gibbs had been born. But he didn't know for sure, and who but he would care?

CHAPTER TWELVE

Rainbow

AUNTIE SADIE STEVENSON laboured slowly home with Jack the Labrador dragging and wheezing in her shadow.

It was three miles across the hot plain from the house on the hillock to the Garrett homestead, a distance too great for a distressed woman of seventy-nine because the journey home made it twice as far. She had not foreseen this slow and sick return because she had expected that Mr Garrett would have been compelled to drive her back to town.

'Yes,' she had been going to say, 'I'm here again, Mr Garrett. Yes, I know your wife has taken the children. Yes, I know that Pan Pacific has arrived. But, no, I am not stepping inside, I prefer to stay here at the door, and this time you will not make me cry. I've cried all my tears; they're all spent.

'This time there is no one to overhear, to limit what I would say. Just the two of us, no children at the back of the house, no wife with her ear to the wall in the next room, and Sunday from the same point of view is an excellent time because your station hands are in Kenyon or farther away.'

Then she had been going to say, 'You have heard of the cross in blood marked on my father's door fifty years ago. It drove me, Mr Garrett, to give my life to Chinaman's Reef for as long as any woman or child stayed. I have honoured that vow. I have been faithful. I can hold up my head and look God in the eye. It drove my father, Mr Garrett, to blow out his brains. If a cross were marked on your door, what would you do?

'Don't laugh too readily, Mr Garrett, don't tell me you're a hard man and my father was a fool. My father was as hard as you. My father was a very hard man. And don't tell me that forty-three men dead by accident underground is a different sort of conscience load from cheating simple countryfolk deliberately of their homes. It is only a matter of degree. When you betray this town what do you destroy?'

Then she had been going to say, 'All the dead ones in the cemetery, even your own infant girl of three years ago, and all the dead ones in the mine, and every memory of every moment everyone of us has ever lived in this town. It's not a hole waiting to be dug, it's not houses and a street and paving stones and trees, it's the living and the dead, and I draw no line between. You turn it into an open cut and you violate their lives or violate their graves.

'Don't tell me, Mr Garrett, that it is out of your hands, that the situation is past recall. You were ingenious in the service of your Company; let us see now how clever you can be for another cause. My father never knew whose blood it was on his door, but it will be different for you. With this knife I spill my blood and mark my cross here. Now, take me home to die. I'm too old to be sewn up again and the doctor is too far. I'll have my six feet of that cemetery and there I'll stay and you will not violate my grave, or a curse will fall on you. We're a suicidal family, Mr Garrett. We're hard.'

So she had come to the homestead, racked with fatigue, unnaturally pale and unnaturally hot, and placed her umbrella against the wall that her hands might be free. Then she raised the knocker and let it drop, three times distinctly, and stepped back.

She had waited, hardening her nerve, but no one came. No one had answered the door.

Garrett had gone too, with his children and his wife. No one was at home. Mr Garrett had gone God knows where.

She could not reach him. She could not touch him. The betrayal was as complete as it could possibly be. Justice had gone from the world. No cut with the knife; no cross of blood on the door. Why should he escape scot-free?

Oh, it was a thousand miles home.

Perhaps they'd find her out there in a day or two, dehydrated, dead with not a mark on her body, dead for no reason that made sense. 'Poor old dear,' they'd say, 'like the elephant she had to wander off to die. Well, that's the end, isn't it? Chinaman's Reef has gone. It died without a struggle; just threw in the towel. If it was bigger than her, it's bigger than us.'

The people with fight had long ago gone to make a proper fight of it out in the world. The weak had stayed because no one had ordered them away. Pan Pacific would thunder into town and Chinaman's Reef would die alone and empty like her.

She should have marched out of the front door instead of the back. She had chased a rainbow and nothing had been there. She should have called, 'Let's fight. Let's block the road. Let's use the language they understand. Of course we can't win, but let's show the world that Chinaman's means something to the families that have stayed. Let them know they drive us out, that we don't slink away, then we can honourably go.'

But that would never be. Not a hand would be raised.

'God,' she cried, 'I'm sure you never meant us to turn the other cheek all the time. Is there honour in weakness, is there virtue in letting the bully have his way? He gobbles up what he takes, ignores the tragedy he leaves behind and alters the story to suit his own image in the public eye, and the world never knows and the bully never understands.

'But why should the people of the town feel as I feel? Can Chinaman's be to them what it is to me? How many have said that Chinaman's is me, that it's here only because of me. Were they pleading with me even then to let them go? Have they stayed not because of weakness but because of loyalty to me? Has it been their way of giving back the love I have tried to give the town for fifty years? Good love from them; blind love from me.

'Have they suffered because a silly old woman wouldn't die?

'Am I the keeper of a prison?'

It was a thousand miles home.

Mrs Muir inserted the key and unlocked her side door, opening it melodramatically an inch or two. Cherry was there, in faded red blouse, tight blue jeans, black walking shoes and paisley headband.

'Glory,' Mrs Muir said, 'it *is* you. I didn't think you'd have the nerve. What are you doing there?'

'Our walk, Mrs Muir. It's way past time. Mum says it's all

right if we take the little kids, too. All together like. Can Normie
come, and the girls?'

'No, they can't. Good heavens, no. What an incredible idea.
No, Cherry, no. You go back home. You and your errands to
my door; haven't you brought enough trouble to this house?
I've got the gun story, all of it; I've got it out of him; how
you twisted it around; aren't you ashamed?'

Cherry didn't know what to say.

'I can't believe it, Cherry Cooper, that you'd let me throw
that rock. To think I blamed my boy and it was you. I wouldn't
be surprised if you broke the public telephone and left that to
him, too. I wonder what else I've blamed him for down the
years!'

'Gee, Mrs Muir.'

'No son or daughter of mine leaves this house until the men-
folk are back in town, especially with you, especially today.
You can see what those brutes have done next door. Doesn't it
mean anything to you? Is that the risk you want to expose my
children to? You go home and tell your mother she's out of her
mind.'

'*Please*, Mrs Muir, don't you understand? Next week we
might all be gone. We mightn't have the chance again. Mum
doesn't mind; she thinks it's a good idea.'

'Haven't I made myself plain? Doesn't English make sense
to you?'

'Just our walk, Mrs Muir, like we always do when it's fine.

'Oh, you mean for kissing and holding hands? Yes, at last I
do understand, but no, Cherry Cooper, go home. You're a bad
influence. You're too old for your years. Your mother should
have her head read for allowing you outside. Or has she thrown
you out as she threw out the man? We saw him; we saw him on
the road; he could hardly stand; they had to hold him up.'

'Look, Mrs Muir—'

'Fat lot of regard she's got for me. "Don't worry," your
mother said, "don't worry, dear; he'll be all right in my care."
If he drops dead now what happens to me? Manslaughter?
Murder? What's the charge? Oh, that's choice, that's rare. She
starts the day with her hateful tongue insulting Normie outside
the Store and ends it by breaking her word. No, I will not

subject my children to the danger of the street, not for her, not for you, not for any reason at all.'

The door shut and the key turned and it was no wonder that Normie had not appeared.

'What danger?' Cherry cried at the door. 'They've gone. They're in the railway yards. They've been gone an hour. The street's been empty since three. All the cars and trucks; everything; all gone.'

The door said back, 'If you think I'd let Normie out of here with you you're mad. Go home.'

'What if Leah can come? What if Shane can come, too? What then?'

'They'll not be allowed. We agreed. Children off the street. We agreed. That's another way your mother's broken her word. And I'll not argue another minute with an impudent chit of a girl.'

Cherry heard the heavy footsteps recede, heard a slam somewhere, and stood appalled. 'Mrs Muir,' she breathed, 'that must have been someone else. How could it have been you?'

The thought of knocking on Shane's door and Leah's door with the same invitation seemed suddenly sick—and it had been such a wonderful idea. Walking off as they always did, a sentimental journey for the last time, Normie holding her hand, Leah being shy, Shane trying to make out he didn't mind (poor Shane), the little kids squealing and teasing and yelling 'snake' when it was a lizard sticking his head out of a hole to catch the breeze. A Sunday afternoon just like any other time but with extra special meaning, every yard of the way specially noted and specially remembered to last for the rest of their lives. It wasn't much to ask and Mum didn't mind.

'You're mean,' she shrilled at Mrs Muir's door, 'saying things like that to me. Normie's no angel either. I never dreamt he'd tell tales on me. By golly, I could tell some tales on him and never blabbed a word. You crumb, Normie Muir, you little crumb, you're not even fourteen. If there was anyone else around I wouldn't look twice at you.' Then she ran for the deserted street where the bulldozer had uprooted trees and dragged fences down and compressed a broad curve of rubble between the crown of the road and the land next door. Pan

Pacific had negotiated that curve, vehicle by vehicle, driven out or towed, across the site of the house that had been swept away. No trouble at all. So easy it was a shame. Stick a man on a machine and he could knock a hole in the world, he could go mad with his machine and knock a million years down. But ask for an hour to build a memory and they tell you you're too old for your years, as if growing up was something you shouldn't do.

'Cherry!'

It was poor old Mum over there with her hand to the gate, looking haggard and old. Peter, too, sitting on the fence kicking the pickets with his heels, waiting for the walk that wouldn't be. What on earth would she have done just then if Mum had not been there? Run off probably, run off somewhere, hidden and cried. But Mum was there drawing Cherry to her with a wry smile that meant she had heard.

'Oh, Mum, the things she said.'

'Yes, dear, but we won't discuss them now. Perhaps we were wrong. Perhaps you'd better take your walk another time.'

'There'll be no other time. *Now*'s the time.'

'Very well, then. Go without Normie. Ask Leah and Shane.'

'I can't go without Normie, Mum. What's the use of going without Normie? Going without Normie . . . No.'

'Aren't we going?' Peter said. 'I want to go for my walk. I want to go now.'

'Cherry does, too, dear, but I think we've picked the wrong time. Different people think different ways. We'll do something else, shall we? Perhaps Cherry will play us a tune.'

Peter was not impressed and Cherry was looking at the ground. 'That Normie told tales on me.'

After a pause her mother said, 'And were they true?'

'He shouldn't tell tales.'

'That depends, you know.'

'It never depends.' Cherry suddenly flared, 'If I told what I knew about him he'd be in gaol.'

'As bad as that? My goodness. He doesn't sound like the friend for you.'

'Don't tease. You know what it's like growing up here.'

'I do, darling, I do. I'm still growing up here.' She looked at

Peter on the fence, that beautiful child, and at Cherry with fire
in her cheeks, and across the distance in her mind to her other
daughters, all three, living in a city from which they never
came home. You lost your kids, that's what parents were for,
but you did like to know they were safe and sound. One day
they sat on fences kicking their heels; another day so soon the
world hit them in the eyes and you were not there. 'Have you
thought of that, Cherry?' she said. 'Mothers and fathers growing up, too? I've grown up a lot today. So don't judge Normie.
Don't judge his mother. Don't judge any of us, please. We're all
under strain. Would you like to take your walk with me; just
the three of us; Peter, you, and me?'

'Oh, Mummy, yes please. Yes please.'

Cherry glared at Peter and sighed, 'Oh, Mum . . .'

'You don't have to, Cherry, it was just an idea.'

'Please, Mummy, please.'

'I thought we might see Miss Stevenson. I think she's had a
bad day.'

Peter jumped down and tugged his mother's hand, but
Cherry said, 'Her!'

'Yes, Cherry. To please me.'

'She walked away. She left us to it and didn't care. She went
walking!'

Peter's tug became a compulsion that Mrs Cooper followed
and she left Cherry standing there. 'We don't need Cherry, do
we, Mummy?' Peter said, but the woman raised her voice,
stumbling on the short rein of Peter's hand, 'Miss Stevenson
might have felt the same as you and picked the wrong time. But
isn't that her privilege? She's seventy-nine. She's lived here for
more than fifty years. If you want to walk, can't she?'

But Cherry had no ear for grown-up tricks with words. It was
mad. How could a wobbly old woman feel the same as a girl
when the in-the-middles had not the vaguest idea? Mrs Muir
was as understanding as a blank brick wall. Mum, too, because
off she went with Peter brightly at her side. It must have been
great to be six, going where you were led as if it were your
dearest wish in the world. That house over there. That silent
house of the Muir's. It looked already abandoned, already like a
tomb, in a couple of lousy hours dying dead after a lifetime of

noise. Normie locked up in it, Shane locked up somewhere else, Leah locked up, and Cherry alone like a shag on a rock at sea.

'Come along, dear.'

Her mother's plaintive call was the last straw and Cherry kicked at the fence like a boy and went aimlessly the other way. It would have been easier if she had been locked up, too. What was the use of feet when there was nowhere to go? What was the use of going when tomorrow the world would be gone? Chinaman's, already, was sinking into the ground.

'Come along, dear.' She heard it as plainly as if her mother had called a second time, but when she looked back the street was empty, silent and unstirring, and Mum and Peter had vanished from view and she was herself outside Elliot's Store at the fringe of the dead end of town. She turned her head knowing what would be there and the curtain moved at the bedroom window down the side. But Leah was locked up all the time in a way; confinement indoors would be no hardship for Miss Purity MacPure; she could meditate or say her prayers. That wasn't fair. Yes, it was. Of course it was fair. Leah Elliot would give an honest girl a pain.

Cherry moved a few yards almost callously to interrupt Leah's view with a wall, to hold on to the solitude that she didn't want but was afraid to lose. Her mood was all wrong to share with eyes. It was odd, like taking off into the air but with feet still stuck to the ground.

The telephone box, stark and red, was a sentinel on guard. 'Do not pass,' it said. 'What lies this way is dead and gone.' All the tumbledown places she had played in as a girl; make-believe dancing, really wild, under the spider-webs festooning the Ballydoon bar, worrying the boys although they didn't leave; make-believe games that lasted for days; Shane ringing the anvil at the blacksmith's forge in rhythms that drove the grown-ups mad; make-believe bread in the bakehouse ovens; make-believe funerals in the wreck of the horse-drawn hearse with make-believe widows rending their clothes as in stories told of olden times; make-believe wars, Normie burning down the Bank of New South Wales in a daring attack that almost cost three lives, hers, Shane's, and his own. And Leah at the edges, aloof, always slipping away.

Cherry lost control.

There had been something special about owning the world, out of the back door a thousand miles and not a fence in the way, out of the front door Normie and Shane at the gate while the piano played, at the end of the street Auntie Sadie the dowager queen, at the end of the road Ronnie Garrett biding his time. You were never alone. People living in other places didn't understand. They didn't, they didn't, they didn't understand. But suddenly doors were locked and manners changed and the world you owned was only a hole.

'Auntie Sadie,' she cried, 'I don't mind. Walk all day. Oh, Mum . . . Wait for me . . .'

Running then, fearing that Mum had walked off the end of the world and left nothing of herself behind for Cherry to hold. She was so confused; it was like spinning in a room of many sides with mirrors for walls, not knowing which were reflections and which was you.

It was odd how Mum was suddenly there looking almost vacant yet almost surprised. Auntie Sadie's verandah, Auntie Sadie's front door, Peter with deep concentration down on his knees tracing an ant trail that wandered from floor to wall, but Mum with a hand to Cherry's sleeve. 'It's all right, dear, do quieten down. I'm not cross with you. Cherry, Cherry, stop it, dear, I'm your mother, not your judge.' Mum drooping and tired and drawn. 'Miss Stevenson worries me. She's not here. Isn't it strange? And look at her garden tramped down needlessly. Did you say it was twelve when she walked away? That's hours and hours. It's such a hot afternoon.' Mum was frowning too much, moving restlessly around. 'She's so frail. Where would she go?'

'Mum, I don't know . . .'

'She often takes a walk, but in the evening after tea, not in the heat of the day. That poor old dear on her own. If she's walking out there she'll die. An hour ago it was still a hundred and two. Peter, off your knees. Cherry, run down to the railway yards, see if Pan Pacific have got involved with her. No, no, that's not a job for you. Go back to the hall, she could be there. We should have cared for it better now that she's old, cleaned the windows and mended the chairs, we should be ashamed.' Mum thrusting her head forward as if her neck hurt. 'She feeds the birds at half-past four, milks the goats at twenty to five, sits down to tea on the hour. Peter, do get up off your knees. She's quaint, the way everything must be done on time. As if it mattered. Cherry, you know these things as well as I. Then suddenly she's not here.' Mum sinking to the edge of the ottoman couch with the sigh that meant her back was sore. 'Oh, Cherry, they ought to put *saint* to her name. She's dead. I feel it in here.'

'No, Mum . . .'

'But what can I do? We'd never find her out there in a year. They've killed her, as if they'd hung her from a tree. Couldn't they have waited until she peacefully died? Like the rest of us.'

The haze in Cherry's mind slowly sharpened. Words and meanings stepped into view. 'Mum, what are you saying?'

Mum eased her neck with a twist of her shoulders.

'Mum, that's not true. What an awful thing to say, You haven't been waiting for her to die.'

Mum's eyes looked dull. 'Not wishing it on her, God forbid, not hoping for it either, just waiting, and fearing it, I suppose; but haven't you ever wondered why a woman like Shane's mother rots patiently here? Or why me? Darling, you're old enough to know how the women feel. The men are different, but it's always been a man's country, for men and for children too young to see past the ends of their noses. Yes, and for her. . . . You've had a wonderful time—in a limited way—but there are more things over that horizon than we can give you here. If people live in places like Chinaman's they must *build*; then there's reason for it all; but we mend roads and darn socks and kill time. That's not the sort of building I mean. I'm withering up, Cherry; I haven't the strength that has kept Miss Stevenson alive. Do you want us all, one by one, to wander out there and die?'

'Mum, don't talk like this. It's not you.'

'It's me, dear; the one you've never noticed around. The one you'll be yourself if you don't get out of here. But you'll go, I'll see to that, like your sisters have gone. Don't weep for this place, darling; don't weep for your childhood. Don't fight for something that's gone. We've put on our show, we've done our bit, and that's irony, isn't it now? No woman would fight for

Chinaman's except to please her, and she's not here, she hasn't seen, she doesn't know. Why do you think we allowed our men to throw away leases that secured our homes for another thirty years? Thirty years more? My God; my child; who wants to fight Pan Pacific? Good luck to them with their great big hole. Hallelujah, I say.'

'Oh, Mum.' Cherry threw her arms around her mother but didn't know why. She was horrified, wanted only to argue and to shout each point down, but instead she held on tightly and breathed, 'Mum, don't suffer so.'

'I wouldn't, darling, except for her.'

Kneeling there, Cherry saw a window as for the first time, afternoon light brightening the room inside, Auntie Sadie's bedroom, Auntie Sadie rising like a ghost behind curtains of lace.

Cherry's fingers turned in claws. 'Mum, Mum, Mum. Didn't you look in her room? She's on the bed.'

Mrs Cooper broke her daughter's hold and sat up straight. Then stood, just as stiffly, just as straight.

'She couldn't be.'

'Mum, she is.'

'She's overheard.'

Cherry had to look away. Her mother's face was more than she could bear; Auntie Sadie's shade was something she didn't want to see.

'Oh my God. How could she be there? The Labrador; why didn't he challenge me? Not a bark. Not a sound.'

The voice that came from within the room was tender and sad. 'It's Jack who's dead, Rose dear, not me.'

Mum stepped from the verandah to the ground like a jointed model made of wood. 'Peter,' she said, 'come home. Peter's gone. Cherry, find Peter and bring him home.' Then she turned back to the house, probably not seeing it, calling in a voice unbearably strained, 'You wouldn't believe me if I told you I don't know what I mean. I don't know whether I mean it; I don't know whether I don't. But I'd never wish you harm.'

Then Mum blundered down the winding path and Cherry called crossly, 'Peter, Peter, Peter, come here. Where have you got to now?'

Peter came round the corner, swinging on the grape vine, wrinkling his nose, his game spoiled, and Cherry grabbed his hand and hurried him away. There were things worse than Pan Pacific; houses falling down and towns turning into holes were second-rate troubles. 'Oh, Mum,' Cherry moaned, 'you should have locked us up. This horrible thing's happened to us because we were outside. It hasn't happened to Normie or Shane, and couldn't have happened to Leah in a hundred years.'

Peter protested alongside, 'Aren't we seeing Auntie Stevenson? I wanna stay.' But Mum out front had arrested her stride, had turned half round and raised a hand. 'Listen,' she seemed to say and Cherry stopped short, bewildered and breathless, feeling like someone knocked repeatedly to the ground. There was a sound, a motor horn, short sharp bursts like a signal from far away coming nearer, bearing down on the other end of town.

'The men,' Mum shrilled, 'the men are home. Grace. Madge. Do you hear? *It's Bill's van.*'

Peter broke away and ran. The door of the Baxter's house opened and Shane and his brothers and his mother came out almost in a heap. Mrs Elliot was suddenly in the centre of the road; perhaps Leah was there, perhaps not. The Muir family emerged in a tight group, defensively it seemed, Normie's shoulder held by his mother's hand, and those plump little girls, oversized for their age, close like bodyguards.

Mum called again, beckoning, 'Cherry, please . . .'

Her feet dragged but she had to go and the van came roaring into town, Mr Muir's head and shoulders hanging out of the side. 'We've licked them,' he bellowed, 'they can pack up and leave. Is everyone deaf? Didn't you hear the public phone?'

Cherry saw Chinaman's like a painting on a wall. Every face she saw in an instant so vivid she'd never live long enough to forget that it came. Shock and joy and pain and incredulous surprise. Normie making a stride before he ran. Shane leaping clear of the road, his mother's face caught with despair. Leah, really there, spinning a circle on her toes. The men piling out opposite the store like heroes home from a war. Cherry's own mother with a hand to her mouth stifling a cry. Mrs Muir as blank as a blank brick wall. And Cherry herself able only to see it, not able to feel as if it meant anything to her, rejecting every detail as impossibly bizarre.

'I said we had rights,' Albert Muir boomed, 'didn't I, but what the blazes has been happening here? Look at my blithering road!'

Cherry shivered and hurried to her mother. Oh, Mr Muir; ten thousand things to shout aloud and out comes that stupid road. *Proved* what Mum had to say.

'Cherry,' Mum said, 'you'll be happy now.' She gave a brief and nervous smile. 'For the life of me I can't imagine what our rights might be. You never know, do you? Life's a constant surprise.'

'Mum, he's only worried about his road!'

'Of course.'

'The hall,' they heard him shout, 'and the Anglican churchyard. They're ours! They can't dig them up, so they can't dig up the town.'

'Mum,' Cherry cried, 'we're not Anglicans.'

'I think we've changed religions, dear.'

The men were marching up the road sweeping children into their arms, Normie in the middle of them, Shane there, Mrs Elliot and Leah like a couple of birds, Mrs Baxter being kissed as she'd not been kissed for years.

Cherry's Dad came running their way with a smile as radiant as a boy's, his voice soft, his words a little strange. Endearments were not really Dad's line. 'Rose, oh Rose, the law's on our side. Bless 'em all. Cherry, you'll not lose your home. Oh, family, Chinaman's is ours for ever and a day.'

Mum was crying, but laughing too, being crushed by Dad. *She looked so happy, so pleased.* They were all together, a bundle tied with arms, Peter yelping because Dad's foot was on his toe.

'You'd never guess through whom. Bless the old girl. Miss Clapp. I think she felt pretty bad. She sent us off to the Shire Historian. Didn't know we had one, did you? He dug it up in an hour.'

Dad was standing there now, still smiling, breathing heavily.

'Why didn't you people answer the phone? We rang and rang. Old Bill's rocketed us home at a fantastic speed. It's a wonder we're alive.'

But Dad's smile was fading as he looked around. 'The trees. The Lindsay house! *Where's it gone?*'

'We fought,' Mum said, 'we had to. We fought, Cherry, didn't we?' Mum gave a funny dry cry. 'You did it your way, I suppose, and we did it ours.'

Dad frowned, not only with his brow but with his eyes and mouth and the wrinkled tan of his neck, and Cherry felt totally lost, as if something had gone wrong with the rhythm of the world. She scarcely knew that everybody else had arrived and that the big voice of Albert Muir was declaring that Pan Pacific had had its bit of fun and had better 'hop it' right now. 'Let's sort 'em out,' he said. 'Treating us like dirt. By the livin' Harry, young Shane, if you'd told us this morning what you'd over-heard. . . . Well, you didn't, did you? We'd gone. Maybe just as well. There'd have been a bloody war.'

CHAPTER THIRTEEN

Crack in Armour

ALBERT MUIR led with an aggressive stride and the people of Chinaman's were drawn behind. He was impressive and wore the confidence he had had as a young man, gladdening his wife's eye. She liked men to be firm, to know their own minds. When her man was in that mood for other people to see she felt ten feet tall. They jostled after him off the street and followed the bulldozer path across the scored earth where the Lindsay house used to be.

'Albert; what are you going to do?'

'The nerve,' he boomed, 'look at our road, look at the fences, take a look at this house. *And* the only orange tree in town! They'll be sorry, the cows. Calling me a bush lawyer. Calling me half-baked. I'll bush-lawyer him. Calling us those things that Shane heard.' He peeled off his jacket as he marched and slung it over his shoulder and started rolling up his left sleeve. He looked back and all were there. It was a moment of power. He looked ahead and wheels and caterpillar tracks and bull-dozer blade had crushed everything down. 'The nerve,' he boomed, 'as soon as our backs are turned.'

Shane kept on calling out, stumbling over the cut-up ground, 'He said he'd empty us out neck and crop. He said he'd pile everything into a heap and set a match to it.'

Normie stumbled too, but was angling to fall back on Cherry, to will her to look his way, but was almost afraid that if she did she might wither him into the ground. 'Strike me, Cherry,' he wanted to explain, 'I feel terrible about it all, but I didn't blab, I don't tell tales. She *forced* it outa me. She's a battering ram. Gets you so flummoxed you don't know whether you're a boy or a girl. You saw her earlier on, screamin' up and down the road. Your Mum's not the same. See. So cool you'd reckon she was mixed up in things like this every day.'

150

'He said we were no-hopers,' Shane yelled. 'He said we lived on charity.'

'No more,' his mother said. 'Say no more, Shane.'

But he tried to get away from her; the mood had him in its hold.

'He said we were up to all the lurks that ever were. What did he mean?'

'Shane! Enough will do!'

They were on their way to the railway yards. They were jumping ruts where rabbit burrows had collapsed under huge rubber tyres. Albert Muir was striding it out, both sleeves rolled up. He was looking away from the house on the hillock, looking deliberately away in case he caught sight of her, wanting nothing from her up there, wanting to do this on his own. When she was around he felt less than life size. 'Has she had anything to say?'

'No,' panted Mrs Muir, 'hasn't stuck her nose out of the door.'

'That's fine.' He thrust a supporting hand through his wife's arm. 'We don't need her.' He glanced to his side, expecting Normie there, but it was Shane striding it out, stretching, trying to make it stride for stride, Shane with his mother on his heels looking so grim that it was not only Albert Muir who misread her state of mind. Grace Baxter looked like a war horse; by the living Harry she did. Shane said, 'They tried to buy me off, Mr Muir. They gave me money and I threw it back at them.'

'That's the boy.'

Shane sniffed with a twist of his nostrils and a twist of his lips and glanced back. He was leading again, cock of the walk, striding it out. It was a good feeling. Leah was back there but who was Leah? She was nothing. He couldn't get excited any more about her. Kissed the ground he'd walked on since he was six. Too bad for her.

Mrs Elliot called, 'The churchyard and the hall. I don't understand. Are you men sure?'

Albert Muir yelled without looking round. 'It's as good as what Pan Pacific's got. It's written down, same as theirs. You'll see, Madge.'

'You'll be feeling sick if it's not what it seems.'

'We rang some bloke in Sydney. The historian gave us his name. That's how sure we're sure.'

There were glimpses of machinery above the scrub line, metal extrusions painted red and yellow catching the afternoon sun. The railway yards were not far. Shane had an eye on them. 'Do you know what else he said, Mr Muir?'

'We don't want to know!' He felt his mother's breath on his neck and the fierceness of her words and rebelled against the injustice of it all. 'Leave me alone,' he hissed, 'or I'll tell them what *you* said!'

'Albert,' gasped Mrs Muir, 'you're going much too hard. We're tired . . .'

'Aren't we all?'

'Do you know what else he said, Mr Muir?' Shane was determined to get through and shook off his mother's hand.

'Please, Albert, do slow down.'

'I'm not stopping now, woman.'

Mrs Muir was distressed and breathless and horribly flushed. 'If you don't slow down you'll leave me dead, I'm afraid . . .'

He stopped, lips pursed with an impatience that entirely possessed him. Sadie Stevenson's house was too close for his liking. She could muscle in on the act in too few strides.

'Mr Muir, he said that women and kids shouldn't have to live in squalor in a country like this.' Shane shouted to make himself heard and his mother grabbed him by the shoulders and shook. 'Stop it, you disobedient boy. I'll not forgive you for this.' Her face almost frightened him. 'Stan Baxter, will you keep your son quiet. He's got a devil in him. Aren't feelings running high enough?'

'We've got the message, Shane. The point's made. Forget it!'

'Don't you want to know?' Shane wrenched himself rudely free. 'Don't you want to know what he said? Someone ought to know.'

'But we do know.'

'You don't, you don't.'

'You've told us, son, and we're as angry as you are. You've said it before and it might have been better if you had not said it at all!'

It was a crisis of discipline, difficult to handle, with the grown-ups striving not to provoke an outrageous scene.

'But Mum doesn't care,' Shane cried, 'I know she doesn't. She locked me in the bathroom without any clothes. I told her then and she wouldn't answer me. She locked me in the bathroom for two hours.'

'Don't twist things, Shane. You were not locked up for that reason.'

'Well why did you lock me up? Why? Why don't you tell them why?'

It was too far gone; there had to be a scene. Shane's father grabbed him by the collar of his shirt and the seat of his pants and frog-marched him away. 'Go without us,' he called, 'we'd cruel your pitch.' Shane could have wept.

Albert Muir swung on his heel, banging his fist into his thigh, in an ugly mood. He didn't like losing a man. That was the price of stopping. He'd stop no more. He carried them on with an impatient surge, Leah looking back, pained, and Cherry aware of the grown-ups and their tensions as never before.

You wouldn't think the women hated Chinaman's, you'd never dream. That flashlight moment of the van's return had unmasked all four, but only for her; not another girl or boy, and not a man knew in the same way. Except perhaps for that Gibbs fellow saying things that Shane repeated like a parrot, Shane not knowing that truth could come dressed in strange clothes. Would a man like Dad force the girl he had married to live where she hated to be? Mum was a smasher in those photo‧graphs on the wall. 'Dad, how could you be so blind? Mum looks so old and she's not old. She's not. She's not.'

Mum striding along in the crowd with her face set like stone, in her cheap dress and her hair *white*. You thought it was gold, but it wasn't gold at all. 'Oh, Mum, you're a fool.'

Mum had opened a crack in the door of the adult world where lives were a masquerade, where women who loved their husbands and their families put themselves last every time. Acting it even now, putting on a show that could be nothing more than a great big ache. 'Gee, people; we're a sad lot, for sure.' How could the women do it every day? Hate the place like poison but never show it? 'Mum, it's not Auntie Sadie who ought to have *saint* to her name. Maybe it's you and Mrs Baxter and Mrs Elliot and Mrs Blooming Muir. Never doing what you want to do. Hardly ever. Putting on a great big act day after day. It's mad. Could I do that for someone? For anyone? For Normie?'

Cherry turned her head and there he was, nailed by her eyes, a guilty-looking boy. Who had given her his shirt to keep off the sun on a sizzling roof, who had kissed her more often than a good girl should allow, and had nearly burnt her to death in the Bank of New South Wales on her twelfth birthday.

Cherry shook her head but held out her hand and Normie leapt to take it. 'We'll show 'em, Cherry,' he said, 'they can't push us around.' Cherry smiled and felt rather old. 'Gee, Cherry, I didn't really tell tales on you.'

'I know.'

'What about Shane? Crikey . . .'

They were at the place where the gates to the railway yards used to be. The steel rails had been carried off as scrap to help fight wars; the sleepers had been sawn into one-foot lengths long ago and burnt to cook thousands of meals. Pan Pacific was there, set up like a regiment.

'The nerve!'

Bill Elliot overtook from the rear. 'Albert,' he said, 'there are things you should know before we bust in here.'

'Bust in! You don't bust in on your own town. They've done the *busting* in!'

Brown tents stood in a row, already linked to an electricity supply. The generator engine throbbed as if it had been there for years. Caravans were parked with awnings raised. Laundered clothes hung from lines. A marquee, part erected, must have had the kitchen on its upwind side because someone called, 'That steak had better be for me.' Men, clothed only in towels about their waists, stood in a queue beside the water tanker; it must have been the bath tent, that odd-looking structure of canvas and poles.

'Do me a favour, Albert,' Mr Elliot said, 'take a breath. You wouldn't be fighting them at all if I hadn't had the Kenyon idea.'

'O.K., O.K.'

'My shotgun; they grabbed it from Leah. Normie's rifle; they've got that, too.'

'*Guns?*' said Albert Muir.

'And you haven't heard the half of it.'

'Guns! Who's kidding who?' He laughed, not because it amused him, but because he needed a rest for his nerves. He could not have expressed it in a more imperfect way. Cherry's mother jumped at him, wagged a finger at him, emotion slurring her words, 'No one's kidding anyone, and we'll do without dramatic performances from you. We tried to stop Pan Pacific and if it's blame you're after, try yourself on for size.' (She glanced at Cherry and seemed to say, 'Yes, you were right. Can you say the same about me?' She took the women in with the same glance, challenging them to agree.) 'He gets told, They all get told, these great big heroes rushing us off our feet. I've had about as much as I can stand. You booming big men fretting about your road. Bother your road. What about your kids? What about your women for a change? What about Sadie Stevenson? You don't even know. You lot come booming in here like conquering heroes but we fought that war, Albert Muir, that war you were talking about. We had the street snarled up for three solid hours. That man Gibbs with a great gash on his head and a crashed car. Your kid and mine up in the chimney-pots with a gun. Leah taking them on single-handed to protect young Shane. You back-pedal a bit on your noise, Albert Muir. It's not your blessed historian who's been fighting for this town and it's not you.'

They had tried to silence her, Albert Muir not knowing where to put his eyes, Mr Cooper pleading, 'For pity's sake, dear,' Bill Elliot, having stirred up a hornet's nest wishing he could vanish, horribly aware of Pan Pacific men dressed in towels scattering for cover and of another with a bandaged head leaving a caravan, the women saying, 'Oh shush; oh shush, Rose,' and Cherry shaking with an awful apprehension that Mum was about to go *too far* and reveal things that men and children were not supposed to know. But Mum had had her say and no one's dream world fell down. Mum had played it with hob-nailed boots on, but she had played the game even when she was good and mad.

'Look here, Rose,' Albert Muir said breathlessly, as if he had been struck a body blow. He hoped his wife might help him, but not a word. 'Bill, is this what you meant? Is *this* what I had to hear?'

Leah's father sounded breathless too. 'In a general way . . .'

The big man shook his head and Auntie Sadie said, 'You should be proud.'

Albert Muir groaned, but not aloud. 'That's torn it; she's here.' His command left him; in an instant he felt it go, felt it flow to her as if at last God had intervened. He wanted to give way to fury, but what was the use if she was around? Gibbs on one side of him, with a bandage on his head and his hands on his hips, and Sadie Stevenson on the other. Between the devil and the deep blue sea. He crunched his fists together helplessly. But when he looked at her she was different. She was dusty and bedraggled like a shabby old woman in a crowd, her face papery and grey, with Grace Baxter supporting her and people parting to let her through.

'Proud, Albert,' she said. 'I don't know what they've done, whether it was good or bad, but I don't care. I'm proud. They made Chinaman's their cause.' But was she speaking to him or to Gibbs over there? He didn't really know. 'That doesn't dishearten you, Albert. That makes you strong.' She took his arm and he had never felt her touch before in quite that way. It was strange, that wire-like grip, as if only bones were there. 'Mr Gibbs, you're early, you know.'

Malcolm Gibbs frowned but no one knew because the bandage covered his brow. No one would have believed that he felt exposed. They saw him only as the Company that had loomed over Chinaman's for eighty years.

'Several weeks early,' she said. 'I'm very cross with you.'

No; she didn't see him that way. Every slow and quiet word was barbed to cut him down to size. He didn't mind. It eased a danger that he feared. Tense men behind him and angry men in front, held apart only by his word.

'Of course you know you can't turn these people out unless they choose to go. You know that, Mr Gibbs, you're too thorough not to know what Mr Muir is going to say. You'd simply hoped we'd never learn. Tell him, Mr Muir.'

They were coming out of their tents back there, dressed, buckling their belts, buttoning their shirts, but Albert Muir was calm. She had cut his command away but built him up again. 'The hall belongs to the people, Mister, and the churchyard belongs to the church. It'll be a funny looking open cut with two half-acre lots high and dry in the middle of it.'

Malcolm Gibbs was suddenly irritated and glared at the old lady and then at the man. 'Where'd you get that load of rubbish?'

'We got it from the Shire, Mister, and rang Sydney to make sure. It's written down, it's all written down. We've got rights.'

But there was a cry in Auntie Sadie's eyes that crossed the gap with Albert Muir's words. 'You know they can't win,' she seemed to say, 'let them down gently.'

He dragged a pipe from his hip pocket and started poking at it and discovered that he was looking at the girl who had pummelled him with her fists and condemned him with her stare. Looking at her, but feeling nothing. 'All right then,' he said unexpectedly, 'we'll have a funny-looking open cut with two half-acre lots high and dry in the middle of it.'

'*Two* half-acre lots?' said Auntie Sadie, sounding surprised. 'That house belongs to me until I die and then I'll have six feet of cemetery. A funny-looking open cut with *three* half-acre lots and six feet of cemetery high and dry.'

'There'll be more than six feet of cemetery,' Owen Cooper growled, 'my old Mum and Dad are out there.'

But it was foolish and Malcolm Gibbs was not in the humour for playing games. 'Miss Stevenson is absolutely right,' he barked, 'I'm too thorough not to know, of course I know.' He was angry with them; were they all children, irrespective of years? 'I could tell you of a few more pieces of land supposedly yours, but not one will stand up in a court of law. Miss Stevenson must know.' He looked at her, astonished. 'There's nothing legally concerning this place she doesn't know. She pulled the church on us years ago and the cemetery's taken care of, she knows that too. The hall's neither here nor there; we could leave it where it stands but we won't have to, it'll go. We're not skating round any edges of the law; we're fair and square down the middle. We owe you nothing. You add it up, you be honest, not a cent. You could spend a hundred thousand in the law courts. Have you got that sort of money? You'd lose.

You cannot seriously believe I would come in here with a crack in my armour that wide. Come now, people, have I got grass in my ears? Am I a thief? Am I a liar? Ask her. Who needs to believe me when she's there?'

He was very angry, pulling his pipe apart and cracking it together again time after time, and he had silenced the old lady; she was not what she used to be. He had silenced Albert Muir into confusion and the men into troughs of misery and the children into sullenness and the women into headaches that spun with words.

'We're not clever,' Cherry's mother said, 'like you. You're big city.'

He glared at her, suddenly alert, remembering her front room.

'I believe you,' she said. 'Goodness me. Would I dare do otherwise?'

'I was born *here*, madam.'

'Were you?' She laughed in that dry way. 'Does that make you a loafer, then? Do you live on charity, too? Are you squalid and dirty? Are you up to all the lurks, whatever that may mean?'

Cherry tugged at her mother. 'Mum, don't . . . He'll get the better of you . . .'

'Mr Gibbs, you might not be a liar, but you're ignorant. You don't know the first thing about *anyone* here. Not even Miss Stevenson. You're not fit to clean her shoes. You bully, Mr Gibbs; you puffed-up little man. Now drive another machine at us. Set your thugs against our boys and girls. Degrade our men with your sneers.'

'Madam, that's not fair!'

'*Fair?*'

He turned away, disconcerted by her scorn, but swung back immediately. 'Mining's in my blood,' He sounded angrier than before. 'I've come here to mine. If I have to change the face of the country why should you complain? We changed it before or Chinaman's wouldn't be here. So we change it a second time. The wheel takes a turn, that's all, and none too soon. Was this place built for a century? Look at it! It was built for a day. I start clean. . . . All right, I admit it. You're not what I believed you were. I apologize.' It was Cherry he was looking for, wanting from her something other than contempt, and Peter the Lord High Executioner, and the girl who had thrown herself at his car; but he found it difficult to focus his eyes. He was not well; his head was like a fire.

'That heap of sticks and stones—it can't stay, it's impossible. What is it that's kept you here?' He went to scratch his head, violently, but the bandage was in the way. 'I don't understand. Haven't you stood back and *looked*? You're not monkeys; you don't live in trees. One house only worthy of the name. We'll jack that house up and move it and plant it again, but the *rest*! I don't know what it is, but if you're determined to stay!' He expelled a breath. 'I want stability in my new town.'

'New town?' It was Cherry's mother again. No one else seemed to be capable of words.

He almost managed to focus his eyes on her. 'A good small town on a railway line, madam, with Company jobs as from now and a thousand people in a year. After that, who can say?'

She gathered Cherry and Peter in with her arms, Cherry an inch taller than her, having to break her hold on Normie's hand, and Peter a long way down. 'What are we supposed to do, Mr Gibbs? Cheer?'

He blinked in her direction.

'*That* was the place we fought for, that heap of sticks and stones. I don't know what the others will say, but we did have dignity, shabby as it might have been. Come along, kids. We're going home until he puts his machine against it and knocks it down.' She turned to her husband, 'Coming, Owen?'

He smiled ruefully and gave a hitch at his belt. 'You mean well, Mr Gibbs, but you see, you don't understand. I reckon my lot will take a crack at Sydney town.'

They didn't have to push out; there was an open way; Normie, round-eyed, knowing that Cherry was going, Cherry was as good as gone, and Leah's gate would be the only one left around. But Dad wasn't going, not Dad; Normie could see that without hearing any words. Mr Elliot wasn't going either; you didn't need a brain to work that one out. But Shane's mother was following the Coopers with one small boy in each hand; the Baxters belonged to Chinaman's, and Chinaman's was gone.

Auntie Sadie said, 'It will be exciting, Normie, for you and Leah, building a brand-new town. I suppose it will be a busy time for me; a thousand people in a year.' But he didn't know whether her face was a smile or a pain. 'How nice your hair looks, Normie, all fluffed up. Leah! Leah, my dear.'